THE LAST OF THE TIME POLICE

THE TIME AUTHORITY
BOOK ONE

Kim "Howard" Johnson

DOUBLE
DARE
BOOKS

The Last of the Time Police
The Time Authority Book One

First Print Edition: January 2014

ISBN: 978-0-9882452-6-6

Cover art: Fantasia Frog Designs

Photograph and model and property:
Canstock-justmeyo
Copyright Gertfrix / Dreamstime
www.dreamstime.com

For Laurie

Chapter One

France 1516

"I'll drive."

The two men threw off the blanket that covered the Time Machine, letting it fall to the floor.

Actually, "floor" was putting it rather generously. Even "mud" was being generous. The stable into which they had rushed so frantically had only occasional lonely clumps of grass on the ground, seemingly swallowed up by manure. A few handfuls of straw had been scattered in a half-hearted attempt to soak up the urine, which collected in puddles on top of the dung.

Both men were far too anxious to notice that someone else had been studying their Time Machine, and had hastily flung the blanket over it when the pair came within earshot. And both were far too concerned with barring the stable door to notice that same figure scurrying into the rafters above.

Together they dove into the third stall on the right, slipping and sliding on the malodorous muck. They had covered the Time Machine upon their arrival, their goal camouflage rather than protection. Then they grabbed a few handfuls of less foul straw from the nearby mangers and carefully arranged it over the blanket. Their original intent had been for the machine to melt into the background, so that any passing stable boy would be oblivious to its presence. In actuality, the result almost seemed to cry out for attention.

As they scrambled, small bits of straw flew into the air. The particles of dust that followed them floated lazily in beams of sunlight that were intruding through the cracks in the wall of the stable.

Jack, the larger of the two men, was already wheezing uncomfortably when he inhaled a cloud of dust. It tickled his nose and the back of his throat, and he tried breathing through his mouth to avoid sneezing.

"You drove last time!" he said, trying to wedge himself into the driver's entrance and block his partner's efforts. "That's why we got into all of that trouble in Alexandria."

Stan, his younger (by six months) partner in the International Time Police Association, acquiesced, but protested as he ran around to the passenger's door.

"I couldn't help it. All of the maps were in Egyptian," he said as he climbed in, kicking as much muck from his shoes as he could manage, which wasn't much. His shoes resembled giant fuzzy slippers made of raw filth. "Why couldn't they just speak English?"

Jack began patting himself down, frantically looking for the keycard that would start the engine. "I don't know," he said to Stan. "Maybe because...it hadn't been invented yet?"

Outside, the soldiers pursuing them had reached the entry to the stable. They began banging on the doors and shouting in French. The thin piece of wood Stan had used to bar the doorway wouldn't stop them for long.

Stan strapped himself into his seat, noticing Jack's frantic attempts to dig through the pockets in his cloak.

"What's the matter? Are you looking for something?" he asked innocently.

"No, I'm not looking for anything," Jack said, imitating his partner with an exaggerated sing-song-y rhythm.

"We better get going. Those soldiers will break through any second."

"I know, I know! I can't find my keycard!"

"It's right here," said Stan, pulling it from his belt in one smooth gesture. "You told me to hang onto it, remember?"

"Give me that thing!" snapped Jack.

Unfortunately, it was at that exact moment that he forgot to breathe only through his mouth. The air tickled the fine hairs in his nostrils and combined with the dust that mingled throughout his respiratory system. The effect was explosive.

"A-a-achoooooooo!"

The violent force of the sneeze startled Stan, who was holding the keycard between his index and middle fingers. He inadvertently jerked, flicked his fingers, and the keycard went flying down near his feet.

Jack's reaction was swift and sure. He dove down to the floorboards and began looking for the keycard. More precisely, he attempted to dive. Too much beer and pasta had robbed him of his feline grace and abilities, and his attempt to lunge to the floor was motivated by sheer panic. He wound up as near to the floorboards as he could manage, which meant that part of him was laying across Stan, while another part was being obstructed by the unit's stabilizer. Still, he could reach the floor with one hand, and so began feeling around for the all-important keycard.

"Gesundheit," said Stan.

Unfortunately for Jack, his partner had tracked a great deal of slop into the time machine, and so he was forced to plunge his hand into it all and feel around for the elusive card.

"Ugh!" muttered the disgusted Jack. "Oh, this is just great."

As he shifted his weight, the stabilizer dug into his midsection and he turned to his right side. Stan immediately responded by turning away from him, and Jack slipped lower, finding both of his forearms immersed in the muck.

"What are you doing?" he snapped.

"You were jabbing me in the knee," said Stan. "Haven't you found it yet?"

"No, I haven't found it yet! If you're not going to help me—"

With a loud splintering crash, the door to the stable burst open. The thin board gave way to five soldiers, armed with an assortment of bows, swords and shields. After a few tentative steps inside, they stopped to examine their surroundings. Large cracks in the walls let in the bright mid-day sun, but the soldiers were still momentarily disoriented.

"You better hurry!" whispered Stan. "They're here."

"Yes, I know," muttered Jack through clenched teeth.

"If you hadn't sneezed—"

Jack looked up from his search, mustering up as much dignity and authority as possible with his upper body covered in pig shit. He shot Stan the most menacing glance he could manage, but it was enough. Stan shut up.

The building contained eight pens, four on each side. Save for the stall that housed the Time Machine, none were occupied by anything larger than a 20-pound rat. The soldiers split into two groups to search each of the stalls, with the senior officer moving as close to the center as possible in hopes of avoiding the stench and the muck.

Both teams of soldiers stationed themselves outside the doors of the two closest stalls. On signal, they each kicked in the doorways. The soldiers on the left saw the wooden gate collapse inward and provide them with a clean, manure-less platform on which to survey the interior. They rushed onto the wooden slats on the floor of the vacant stall and looked around, swords drawn. The pair of soldiers on the right were not as lucky. As they kicked in their gate, it dropped down, and then fell backward, directly onto them. Though it wasn't heavy enough to hurt them, they were both knocked off their feet and into the excrement.

All the while, Jack frantically clawed through the slop at Stan's feet. Stan ducked in a futile effort to avoid the search that he knew was coming, when a reflective glint caught his eye. He reached between his seat and the door and pulled up the keycard.

"Got it!" he whispered triumphantly, then leaned down to whisper to Jack. "We'd better get going."

"What are you—" Jack looked up with a mixture of relief and anger. By now, even his face was smudged with dung. He saw the shiny, clean card in Stan's shiny, clean hand.

"I better start it," said Stan. "Your hands are all muddy."

He plunged the card into the slot and pressed the Engage button.

"That's not mud," muttered Jack as he climbed back into his seat.

As the Time Machine sputtered to life, the nearby soldiers immediately took notice. None of them had ever heard an engine of any sort, as the only engines that could have operated in that region of France in the early 16th Century were from other time machines. No one wanted to be the first to turn tail and run for fear of losing a pension or a favorite appendage, and so the soldiers gathered together. The turbines wheezed and chugged loudly as the soldiers cautiously approached the stall. With a few gruff words by their commander, the men cut the rope and lifted the latches on the gate, prepared to exercise the better part of valor if the strange mechanical beast sprang at them.

Suddenly, the great *pockety-pockety* roaring stopped.

The abrupt silence alarmed the soldiers even more, though not as much as it worried Jack and Stan. Seated before the control panel, they scrambled to start it up again before the soldiers overcame their fears and dragged them off for some old-fashioned 16th Century torture. Neither remembered much of the history instruction that was a required part of their Time Police training, but the lecture on "Torture through the Ages" —always well-attended—remained vivid. All of the students were riveted to descriptions of thumbscrews and red-hot pokers, as well as some of the more creative but lesser-known instruments of pain. Safe in their climate-controlled lecture hall, few of them could imagine thumbscrews and red-hot pokers, or being on the receiving end of a molten lead enema. As their engine stubbornly refused to start, however, Stan and Jack needed little prodding to envisage their fate.

"Come on, Nellie!" urged Jack.

In front of them, the gate fell to the ground. A head poked around from one side and peered into the stall. Two, three, then four heads followed. Each pair of eyes were wide, but quickly grew hostile. From a safe distance away, their commander barked an order in Italian. The men stepped forward with swords drawn and blocked the gateway.

Jack pounded the instrument panel as he pushed the Engage button once again.

"Try the blue button," suggested Stan.

"That won't work!" snapped Jack.

Four soldiers were attempting to block their path. They seemed larger, more of a threat than they had a moment ago. Desperate but reluctant to lose face, Jack reached over and pushed the blue button. The craft began sputtering to life.

"Good girl, Nellie!" said Stan, nodding with a self-satisfied grin. They both preferred the friendliness of "Nellie" to the colder and more cumbersome "NLE-13," which was the official name and model number of their craft.

The soldiers looked at each other and took a step back. Another order from their unseen commander (who, unbeknownst to them, had backed even further away when the sputtering began) urged them forward. Mustering up the courage, they slowly but surely brandished their weapons and eased forward.

The turbines kicked in at full power now, but the soldiers were getting their confidence back. The four of them surrounded the Time Machine and raised their swords. One of them shouted an order to surrender that went unheard by Stan and Jack.

"I think we'd better get out of here," said Jack nervously.

"Ooooo..." moaned Stan as he began pushing buttons, looking at the soldiers surrounding them.

At that moment, several things happened simultaneously. The largest—and truth be told, the stupidest—soldier cocked his arm back as he prepared to swing his sword at the Time Machine. Startled at the commotion below him, the man in the rafters, who had been observing the entire encounter, fell directly on top of the Time Machine. The large soldier stepped back for a moment, puzzled by the falling man. Hearing the noise and fearing the squad was attacking, Stan pushed the Transport button.

Nellie began to fade from sight. Not willing to let this curiosity escape so easily, however, the commander ordered his men to attack. The four men grew more courageous as the ship continued to fade, and charged it with swords held high. The large—and stupid—soldier took a powerful swing. The sword sliced deeply into the skull of the commander, who had somehow slipped in front of him. Unfortunately, the craft had already faded away, and Stan's final glimpse of the 16th Century was the contrite, stunned face of the large soldier.

Chapter Two

Digression

Soon after time travel was developed, the need for some sort of regulation became apparent.

In the early days of time travel, the problems were somewhat predictable. After the first test runs traveling a few days backward into the past, every time traveler coincidentally returned to find himself a millionaire lottery winner. The number of test subjects became rapidly depleted, because each of them resigned after their first trip. And just as coincidentally, their first trips immediately preceded their lotto wins.

By the fourth test, the luster of the program had faded. One of the last remaining time travelers, a well-intentioned young man named Wilson, agreed to pick up a few lottery tickets for his fellow workers. It was the same week that the $2 million lottery prize was divided among 415 winners, all of whom were friends, relatives or co-workers of Wilson. Suspicions were raised. The winners were unsympathetic as well, as each of them would collect only $240 each year for the next 20 years.

It soon became obvious to that this time travel business was a bit trickier than the government had thought.

The biggest worries centered on scientific expeditions to prehistoric times, where stepping on a butterfly could eventually prevent the human race from developing. At least, that was the theory. Scientists were unable to put it to the test in any sort of non-catastrophic situation. Not until the next decade, when the Time Authority had been established, was a method developed to detect time disruption.

The Time Stream was discovered to be not unlike a water stream. Time, like water, flowed along its regular course until disrupted by some outside force. In the case of water, it could be as insignificant as a stone being thrown into a stream, causing a splash and a few ripples with no long-lasting effects, or as significant as a dam completely blocking the water and forcing it to flow along a completely different path. Time disruptions could be as minor as a few unscheduled lottery winners or as ominous as stepping on a small prehistoric mammal and making the ostrich the dominant species on the planet. In either case, the closer the disruption to the point of origin, the greater the likelihood of some significant change. So, just as the ripples in a stream can be spotted before they hit the shore, the ripples in the timestream could be spotted from the present and—hopefully—eradicated before they could reach and alter the present.

Once the equipment was refined and capable of spotting time anomalies, the scientists' impeccable logic dictated that the most efficient way to rectify the Time Line was with more time travelers. The authorities began organizing and training a group of individuals who would be sent back in time, to correct or eliminate those anomalies.

The "Lotto Fiasco" notwithstanding, most of these early "timenauts" (as they were dubbed by sycophantic co-workers hoping to be cut in on the lottery action) were rather effective at their jobs. Aside from the odd UFO sighting or an occasional extinction, there were apparently no major disruptions since the inception of time travel. And a good thing too, since one mistake could have obliterated everything that followed. Because of this, and because of the tremendous cost associated with the program, the authorities began to strictly regulate each journey to the past. And one incident had them seriously considering the elimination of time travel altogether.

Time travel had been kept out of the hands of the private sector after an attempt to license individual trips to industry proved disastrous. One American telephone company bought a trip to the past and promptly took actions in the early 20th century to eliminate every other competing telephone company.

As a result, that company established a monopoly on telephone service that, for contractual reasons, could not be undone. The public had to live with it, but as they didn't know any different, accepted it with a minimum of complaints.

Problems caused by the original timenauts had been straightened up as much as possible. Without tremendous government money for research and development, the entire line of time machines began to fall into disrepair just months after they had been built. There had been some talk of funneling funds from the defense budget to keep the project going, but as luck would have it, the election was fast approaching, and no politician with a prayer of staying in office dared be perceived as soft on defense. And because the public had not yet been made aware of this innovative use of their tax dollars, there seemed no other choice but to let the Time Travel program grow dormant.

When rumors of the impending closure started flying around the lunchroom at the Time Authority, several of the timenauts immediately resigned. A few more hung on, hoping to make a lotto killing, but were thwarted when security personnel searched their belongings upon their return. Oddly enough, those same security personnel resigned shortly after, and became lotto winners themselves. At any rate, the Time Authority began losing employees at a rapid clip.

Just before it was scheduled to shut down entirely, only two timenauts remained.

Time travel, and science in general, did not come easily for Stan Keaton and Jack Wilson. They both had to study three times as much as their classmates to be judged worthy of admission to the Time Authority. Stan's uncle, a dim but personable congressman, had managed to "pull a few strings" to ensure that his nephew was admitted (one of his final acts before an alleged shoplifting incident at an adult movie theatre led to his resignation from Congress). Jack was able to join the T.A. due to an unfortunate clerical error; by the time it was discovered, he was allowed to stay for fear of embarrassing the Admissions Office.

The pair found themselves working together to survive the rigors of the program. At first glance, they could not have looked more different. Stan was tall and thin, with an unruly shock of reddish hair that seemed precariously balanced on the top of his head. He was pleasant, genial, and accommodating—a perfect partner for Jack.

Jack was larger than Stan, more big-boned than heavy, but despite his size, he was courtly and precise in his movements. He liked to think of himself as a ladies' man, yet a smile from a pretty girl never failed to set him stammering.

Stan and Jack were not the brightest, nor the most competent of the timenauts. According to many at the Time Authority, quite the opposite was true. Their earnestness and desire to succeed were, unfortunately, not matched by their abilities. Still, they were deemed good enough for the job when only one mission remained on the last functioning time machine before the financial plug was to be pulled, and the number of active timenauts had dwindled to two.

It was to be a routine hop to the Mesozoic Era to pick up a discarded chocolate bar. One of the members of an earlier expedition had left it on a rock, and it was eaten by a prehistoric mammal that was an early ancestor of the dog. It soon fell sick and died, and as a result, the only dogs to evolve were yapping little Pekinese. While this did not appear to be a major disruption in history, the nasty-tempered canines were judged too annoying to tolerate. So Stan and Jack were sent into the mists of pre-history to pick up a Chunky bar.

The pair were judged to be capable of meeting this challenge, and it should have been a routine mission. They located the lethal chocolate without much difficulty and snatched it off the ground unscathed. Disaster was averted, and the prehistoric mammal had no idea how close it had come to a history-altering death. Stan's enthusiasm for "seeing a real dinosaur" was dampened rather quickly by the unanticipated arrival of a fierce, 18-inch lizard that sent them scampering back to the Time Machine. So frightening was its sudden appearance that Stan had to be restrained from hurling the chocolate at it in his rush to escape.

As they fired up the Time Machine, Jack snatched it from his hand. His mouth began to water, and as the tempting chocolate rested in his palm, he began mulling over possible excuses to eat it.

All the while, the Time Machine continued its journey. Had either been a trifle more philosophical, they might have mused on how something that seemed so awe-inspiring and miraculous only a year before had become dull routine. Granted, there was not a great deal of visual stimulation in a voyage through space and time. The entire process was manipulated through their instrument panel, and most of that was automated.

There was a bit of shimmering at first, both for the timenauts looking out at the environment and for the residents of that era who happened to see the Time Machine. Both began turning transparent in the others' sight before finally disappearing altogether.

For the timenauts, the outside environment faded to an ugly grey-green mist. Unlike movies or comic books, there were no long tunnels with colored lights or artistic montages of the seasons changing or pages falling from a calendar during the journey, which disappointed many of them. Instead, there was a series of slight but continuous vibrations as their craft seemed to hover in the ether. Only an instrument reading gave the precise day, month and year, along with the correct latitude and longitude, as the craft allowed them to travel through space as well as time.

It was that instrument which was to prove useful in correcting their error.

Tucked away in his hand, Jack surreptitiously moved the chocolate bar close to his mouth until Stan spotted him.

"Hey, I want a bite," protested Stan, his voice buzzing ever so slightly due to the vibrations of the craft. He reached over to pull the chocolate away from his partner's mouth and a brief struggle ensued. Jack was determined that if he couldn't have it, neither could Stan. He gave a fierce tug, and the chocolate flew out the side of the craft, landing in 16th Century France.

Both looked sheepish, and an indicator light began flashing to determine a possible anomaly. The two trained professionals snapped into action.

"It wasn't my fault!" they exclaimed in near-unison. They were not strangers to such incidents.

Looking at the aforementioned instrument panel, they noted their time and space coordinates, and proceeded to pull the time-traveling equivalent of a U-turn. Their instruments directed them to a small villa in the French countryside early on a warm autumn evening in October 1516. Fortunately for their mission, they materialized next to a stable, out of the sight of everyone but a pair of nonplussed horses and a curious but hidden old man. They carried their craft inside and hid it under a blanket and straw, wrapping additional blankets around themselves to more adequately blend into their sloppy surroundings in case they were spotted.

After a few minutes spent combing the immediate area, Jack—who by now had worked up a real taste for chocolate— spotted a silvery glint. The Chunky bar had landed in a muddy furrow that was half-filled with standing water. At least, it might have been water, but with the cattle and horses nearby, even Jack preferred not to take the chance.

"All right, you'd better grab it," said Jack.

"Me? Why me? I didn't drop it—"

"Come on, don't be such a baby," scolded Jack.

"Don't know why I always have to do the dirty work," Stan muttered to himself.

Using a corner of his blanket, he reached over and retrieved the chocolate as though he were handling toxic waste. He picked up the dripping candy and dropped it into the plastic bag that Jack held out. At the same moment, both of them noticed, to their mutual surprise, that the blanket was actually wrapped around Jack.

"Oh...um..." said the genuinely surprised Stan.

Jack began to speak, but stopped and simply shook his head slowly.

"Let's just get going," he said, and they started back to the stable.

1516

There was no doubt—the Old Man was stranded.

His coach had broken an axle, so he dispatched both of his servants to the last large city they had passed—about a day's ride back—for repairs. In the meantime, he hiked into the nearby French village and took a room at the only inn he could find. He sat by the fireplace in the quiet inn, alone and unrecognized, sketching for hours at a time, breaking up his days with walks around the town square each morning and afternoon.

After three days, the Old Man became annoyed. What he first viewed as a relaxing break in a quaint, leisurely town had turned into growing frustration; everything that had once appeared charming had become tedious. Salai and Battista were normally quite adequate servants, but the longer he was stuck, the more he questioned their competence.

As if the sheer boredom wasn't enough, the Old Man was also late for his first meeting with his new patron. Just his luck, he sighed. Ever since his previous patron, Giuliano, had died, things had gone from bad to worse. Giuliano's idiot nephew Lorenzo suggested that he take over his uncle's sponsorship, and the Old Man had to pretend to hear him out. He had inherited a healthy chunk of his uncle's scudi, but Lorenzo was a moron. Still, money is money, and so he seriously considered the possibility until Lorenzo began describing his plan to have the Old Man paint all of the statues in Rome. At that point, the

Old Man feigned a coughing spell and his servants ushered him from Lorenzo's chambers. He immediately sent out a dispatch to France in search of a new job. Things in Italy were becoming entirely too competitive anyway, and he wasn't as young as he used to be. Too many snot-nosed kids were coming along, hoping to become the Next Big Thing; they were all anxious to step into his shoes, and didn't care if they had to chop off his feet to do it.

As he was kicking around the village square for what seemed like the hundredth time in three days, the Old Man began toying with the idea of heading to Paris on his own. He hadn't traveled alone in years, but the longer he stayed in this flea-bitten village, the more it seemed worth the risk. He could be no more than two days' ride from Paris, and so he determined to head over to the largest stable in the village to hire a coach and a horse.

But twenty feet from the stable door, the air shimmered, and the Old Man ducked out of sight. Something was materializing before him, a rather shiny, spindly coach with two men sitting inside. They spoke in a strange language and appeared to be annoyed with each other.

The pair carried the strange coach inside the stable. He waited until the two strangers departed, then slipped into the stall to examine their craft more closely.

The Old Man was puzzled. There were no wheels, no cranks or levers, no animals to pull or otherwise power it, and he could see no recognizable turbines or engines.

He began pressing buttons. When those proved completely unresponsive, he grabbed a small splinter of wood from the stable wall and tried to pry the cover off the instrument panel. When that proved resistant, he tried poking the stick into the slot for the Activation Card.

There was no response at first, and then suddenly the digital panels lit up. Unbeknownst to him, this would become a very popular technique among teenagers born a few centuries later for hot-wiring cars.

The Old Man was so startled he dropped the stick and jumped back. The instruments went dead once again. The Old Man stepped forward cautiously, picked up his stick and tried it again. After another 30 seconds, he was rewarded again as the panel came to life. This time, he didn't jump back. Instead, he bravely pushed a button.

"DO YOU WISH TO RE-PROGRAM DEFAULT SETTING?" flashed the question on the LED screen.

For the Old Man, the question might as well have been written in Navajo. But undeterred by his ignorance, he pushed another button.

"DEFAULT MAY BE RE-PROGRAMMED AT THIS TIME. PLEASE ENTER DATE AND/OR COORDINATES," was the cooperative message that now flashed before him.

Out of curiosity and also out of frustration, he began pressing more buttons, waiting for something interesting or enlightening to happen. Aside from a few "INVALID COORDINATE" and "PLEASE RE-ENTER DATES," it responded readily to his probing.

Suddenly, the sound of a few angry shouts interrupted his experimentation, so he escaped in the only direction he could—up into the rafters. He wriggled up with surprising agility, wrapping his legs around a support beam for additional safety. He watched wide-eyed as the pair burst into the stable below and tumbled into their coach.

From his perch, the Old Man felt splinters digging into his legs. He tried shifting his weight to relieve his pain. He slipped as the soldiers burst in, and he began kicking and flailing as he tried to regain control while remaining out of sight. He might have even succeeded in wriggling back up had a horsefly nearly the size of his thumb not taken the opportunity to bite his cheek. As he attempted to slap the insect with one hand, he fell onto the coach just in time to see his surroundings fade from view, and the sputtering chariot carried him off through the Mists of Time.

Chapter Three

The Mists of Time

The NLE-13 was notorious for its less than reliable operation. For that reason, it was only sent on the most routine of missions.

Although their co-workers would never admit it, Stan and Jack were likewise notorious for their less than reliable operation on the most routine of missions. And their present mission was nothing if not routine.

It was the unscheduled arrival of the Old Man on top of the NLE-13 that transformed the operation into a flat-out catastrophic.

Nellie chugged her way through the Time Stream, as the Old Man clung to her top with his last ounce of desperate strength. Stan and Jack bickered inside, oblivious to the drama that was playing out just above their heads. Nellie was designed and built for two average-sized adults, and a third person on the roof threw off her stabilizing units. She began to shimmy and shake—slowly at first, but rapidly becoming the time-traveling equivalent of a bucking broncho. The Old Man clutched the small rooftop homing beacon for dear life as he repeatedly slammed into the top of Nellie, so much so that even Stan and Jack finally took notice.

"I think we need to make another emergency stop," noted Stan. "Sounds like something is hitting the roof."

"Where are we?" asked Jack nervously as he tried to line up coordinates.

"Looks like 0.00-degrees longitude and 0.00-degrees latitude," murmured Stan, "And...it's the Year, uh...Zero."

"That's the Default Setting, you idiot!"

Unfortunately, the Old Man's meddling with the instrument panel had left all of their readouts indicating 000000. Even worse, they were all blinking insistently, waiting in vain to be re-programmed.

Jack rolled his eyes nervously. Every time he had ever re-programmed the instrument panel it had ended in disaster, and he knew he was more accomplished at it than Stan.

"Get the Operator's Manual," he said slowly and deliberately. "Then hand it to me."

The shaking was getting worse and the thumps overhead were getting louder as Stan rifled through the nearest thing Nellie had to a glove compartment, past centuries-old sticks of gum, yellowed and crumbling maps, and an ancient Egyptian fetish doll to which had been attached a porcelain Betty Boop head.

Reaching to the very bottom of the compartment, Stan pulled out a battered old copy of the NLE-13 Operator's Manual and held it up in triumph. Thankfully they had insisted on bringing an old-fashioned paper printout of the Manual, thought Jack. The way Nellie was acting, they'd probably never have been able to download an e-copy.

As the shaking grew worse, Jack's eyes seized upon the paperback and quickly grabbed for it, making just enough contact with the spine to knock it from the hand of a surprised Stan and sending it flying out the window.

The pair watched in dismay as their only chance to get home sailed into the ether. Their horror increased as it bounced off a foot outside, and a muffled snap came from overhead. Immediately following the NLE-13 Operator's Manual into the Mists of Time was an old man, still frantically clutching their rooftop beacon as he quickly faded from sight.

"Stop! Stop this thing now!" screamed Jack, as visions of home, hearth and an early bedtime dissolved before him.

"I can't! You've got the controls!" cried Stan. "Youwantedtodrivesolletyou! Ididn'tknow! Thebookisgone! Idon'tknowhowtofixit!"

This was Stan's normal reaction to hysteria. While it was a healthy outlet for Stan, however, it only increased Jack's anxiety level. Jack was torn by three simultaneous, paradoxical thoughts:

1) They had to stop the time machine immediately and go back into the recent past and find the Old Man—and the Operator's Manual—or they wouldn't be allowed to return to the future.

2) However, they couldn't go back into the recent past and find the Old Man and the Operator's Manual without first traveling back to the future and getting another Operator's Manual.

3) But neither of them could possibly reprogram Nellie and find their way back to the future without an Operator's Manual.

Jack decided that the only way to pull the time-traveling equivalent of a "time out" was to stop their craft immediately. He began pushing buttons frantically, trying to (literally) freeze them in time. But the button pushing quickly turned into cursing and pounding on the console. Not until Jack reached underneath and ripped out a handful of wires did they lurch to an abrupt, alarmingly silent stop.

Immediately disconnecting the main power cable (which is precisely what Jack's flailing had accomplished) during an actual Time Hop was a risky proposition. Just how risky was uncertain, as no one had ever done it and returned. Nellie was equipped with a wide variety of safety features to ensure that they wouldn't suddenly materialize inside a chunk of granite or at 30,000 feet in the air. But disconnecting the power cable also disconnected most of those major safety features, which is why Stan and Jack materialized in front of a large bat-winged creature flying directly toward them.

The Near Future

The Corporal lined up his putt, as a hush came over the gallery. There was a gentle, almost imperceptible slope to the right. Most people wouldn't even notice, but Corporal Frank Spumoni wasn't like most people, he thought to himself. This was the most important shot he had ever attempted, perhaps the most important shot of his life, but Frank was as cool as a cucumber. He knew about that tiny slant to the right, knew that he only needed to concentrate on his follow-through to sink this one. That's why he was a sure bet to win at Augusta next year, when the Army would only be a distant memory, a far-off reflection in Frank Spumoni's rear-view mirror.

Ever so slowly he drew his wrists back, a couple of inches farther back than the golfing magazines recommended. He knew what worked for him, and that's what was important. He held his breath, and the head of his putter swung toward the ball—

EEEEEEEEEEEEEEEEEEEEEEEEEE!!

The alarm signal startled him, and his golfing fantasy was dashed to bits. The ball went wobbling under a chair to the right, and the putter clattered to the ground.

"Shit!" he muttered. "False alarms!"

Frank picked up the putter and propped it against the wall. There had been two false alarms in the past month, and now this. He walked over to the keyboard and entered the access code. He typed in the disarm information, but the alarm continued. He repeated the disarm, but the irritating noise persisted as loudly as before.

No problem. There couldn't possibly be another anomaly. There was only one Time Hopper still on duty. It was expected to report back any time, and the NLE-13 was on its final mission before the whole operation was shut down.

The military was in charge of the cleanup operation, including the monitoring station, and Frank had spent almost two months practicing his putting and (occasionally) reporting false alarms. It had been the best two months of Frank Spumoni's life. Granted, it was a little boring at first, until he learned the parameters of the situation. There were no taxing physical activities, no strenuous mental challenges. Just a box of documents to file every morning, and the rest of his day was basically free as long as he stayed in the small control room. Frank had gotten so adept at handling the paperwork that he usually finished in about an hour, leaving him seven hours to read the newspaper, eat lunch, (occasionally) nap, and practice his putting. It was a dream assignment. If recruiters could put Frank's smiling face on their posters, enlistments would skyrocket.

But the longer the alarm sounded, the more agitated the easy-going Corporal became. He tried another configuration, then another, but the alarm continued to shriek. If he couldn't stop it, he would have to report to Colonel Hall, who was the de facto boss around here. The Colonel had been ordered to seize control from Mr. Hodges, who was the highest-ranking executive to survive the purge. Hodges was being kept around to turn out the lights when the final timenauts returned. At that point, Frank would have but a few months to shave a few more strokes off his game and turn pro after his much-anticipated discharge.

As the alarm blared, that day seemed further away than ever. For a moment, the Corporal considered shutting off the power and letting the entire system re-load. That might stop it, but if it didn't, he would have to explain the power cut and the alarm.

This was ridiculous. It was obvious, perfectly plain and simple to anyone with a brain, that it was a false alarm, Frank thought to himself. He knew that to let in the slightest fraction of doubt, the tiniest possibility that it was real was to blow his whole comfortable world to shreds. If he even had to inform Colonel Hall—

And then it all came bursting through his defenses, all of his doubts, his fears, and his self-confidence. He couldn't stop it because maybe, just maybe, it was real—not a false alarm or a mechanical failure or an alarm malfunctioning. No, it could be the Real Thing. The Fabric of Time itself might be unraveling, the present-day universe as they knew it might be coming to an end, and he could have to delay his professional golfing career a good six months.

The Corporal picked up the phone to report the onset of the Apocalypse.

Chapter Four

Mists of Time

It was the first time the Old Man had ever journeyed into the future, so his confusion was understandable. It looked as though the entire world around him—all but the mysterious coach below him—had vaporized into nothingness.

He clung frantically to the tiny rooftop beacon, fearing that he too would be lost if he slipped off. After a few moments, he relaxed enough to examine his surroundings. The smooth, shiny metal on the top of the coach made it impossible to find a handhold. He considered reaching down along the sides in hopes of a more secure grip, but feared losing his grip on the beacon. It was a small projection no more than three inches in diameter and half an inch high. A small curly wire was sticking out of the top, a foot-long wire that the Old Man was trusting wouldn't snap. He didn't know that it allowed travelers to remain in contact with the future, and had little else to do with the operation of the craft. Of course, the Old Man couldn't know that he was traveling through space, let alone time. The craft below him didn't shimmy or shake—at least not at first, and the only vibrations emanated from the engine chugging noisily below.

The Old Man had an artist's eye for details, yet he couldn't discern any movement, no sense of moving forward, backward, up or down. It was always his fondest wish to fly. He used to sit and watch birds soar through the sky, carefully observing and sketching, even dissecting their dead bodies in hopes of discovering the secret behind their mastery of the air. Eventually he focused his attention on bats to incorporate what he could learn of their movements. But if someone had told him at that moment how he had far surpassed any bird or bat, his reaction would have been stunned disbelief.

He could only see the grey mists around him and feel the engine chugging below. He could hear the two men beneath him, riding comfortably in their seats rather than hanging onto a few inches of twisted wire. Though fluent in both Italian and French, his English was crude, and he could only pick up a few scattered words and phrases. The two were arguing with each other, a disagreement that soon escalated into shouting, with an occasional moment of terror thrown in for good measure. The Old Man clearly heard the phrase "Default Setting," and he paused just long enough to wonder why that phrase somehow sounded so familiar.

Though he couldn't know it, his added weight was making the craft top-heavy. The engine had been vibrating since the mysterious journey began, but now the entire vessel was starting to shimmy and shake to an alarming degree. It was becoming more difficult for the Old Man to hang on. More than once he found himself bouncing a few inches into the air, and then being slammed down onto the roof again, all the while clutching the twisted wire.

As the shouts below him reached a crescendo, the Old Man slipped to the starboard side, hanging onto the homing beacon for dear life. Before he could right himself, a small, shiny square object came flying out of the craft, striking him on the leg. As he inadvertently jerked his leg, recoiling in pain and surprise, the homing beacon snapped. The Old Man maintained his grip on it as he fell from the roof of the craft, slipping off into the dark Mists of Time.

The Near Future

Colonel Lonnie "Long" Hall slammed down the telephone.

"Something wrong, Colonel?" asked Betsy.

"Dammit, I can't trust that shit-for-brains Corporal to do anything!" barked Colonel Hall.

"Colonel, that vein in your forehead is popping out. You'd better relax—"

Colonel Hall pushed his chair back from his desk. His attractive redheaded assistant fell from his lap as he stood up.

"I AM relaxed! Do I look tense? This has nothing to do with tension."

The unruffled Betsy climbed to her feet, efficiently brushing the wrinkles from her skirt.

"No sir, of course not, but you have a meeting with Mr. Hodges in fifteen minutes—"

"Cancel it!" snapped the Colonel, then furrowed his brow and muttered conspiratorially. "I'll tell you who's going to look tense. That miserable General Lewis, that's who. He promised me this was going to be a routine mission!"

"Are you talking about that Time Machine business?"

"That's top secret!" he scolded, then relaxed. "We got a call from Corporal Spumoni."

Betsy stared, uncomprehending.

"The Corporal at the monitoring station?" he prodded.

Betsy nodded in recognition.

"The shit's hit the fan, and nobody knows why," he explained. "The alarm went off, but the coordinates don't track."

"But they're in our last Time Machine! Can't you do a search from this end?"

"There's nothing to search for!" he said. "It's like they all just disappeared from the time line. According to our instruments, they never existed. Bet they wish I'd sent a couple of my men back there, instead of those two timenut losers... Coupla Green Berets back there could take care of any pissant dinosaurs. Blast 'em to extinction a few years ahead of schedule!"

"But can't you just forget about the timenauts?"

"They caused a mess back there somewhere. And it's getting bigger all the time. There's no way to clean it up, and it's headed right for us. Today. 'Chronological Apocalypse' is what they call it. And as soon as it catches up to us, we'll all be gone."

"Gone? Gone where?"

"It isn't 'where.' It's not even 'when.' We just won't exist anymore. None of us. Everything will be wiped out, or at least changed so much it'll be unrecognizable to people in our time line. It'll be like we never existed—because in the new time line, we won't."

"But what can we do?"

"Not a thing. The only people who even have a chance of correcting it are those two timenuts. But neither one of 'em could find his ass if it had a bell on it. There's gotta be a way for me to do some damage control..."

"You can't dump some of it on the General, can you?"

"No, he knows—Hodges! That's it! I'll drop this ball in Hodges' lap before it gets out. Wormy little bastard. Serve him right. This is his mess in the first place. Serve him right for letting the Army take it over," said the Colonel. "Cancel his cancellation. If this is the end of the world, I won't let the Army take the blame."

Chapter Five

1761

The Old Man landed abruptly on the cobblestone pavement. Despite the distance and time he had just traveled, the effect of his fall was no worse than the tumble he would occasionally take from his dining room chair after a few hours in his cups. There would be a nasty bruise on his thigh and a stern admonition to himself the next morning, though the latter would be forgotten long before the former had faded.

But his current situation appeared to be more serious.

As the mists faded around him, the Old Man had a clearer look at his surroundings. He was on the outskirts of a large city, the likes of which he had never before seen. The stone bridge in the distance looked very familiar, and he knew he had seen it—or at least a woodcutting of it—somewhere, though he couldn't place it. The rest of the cityscape was a bit more puzzling. The architecture was different from anything he had ever seen, and the Old Man decided the situation warranted a closer look. He was still a good distance from the heart of the city, but his curiosity won out over his caution.

He looked around one last time and spotted the NLE-13 Operator's Manual that had struck him on the leg during his fall. On a whim, he stuck it in the pouch inside his robe, and began walking toward the city.

Before he had advanced much further, he saw a coach coming toward him. He didn't know whether to hide, or to question the occupants about his whereabouts. Ultimately, he did neither, and continued walking, doing his best to appear to ignore them, while surreptitiously checking out the carriage and the people inside. Their arrogance and superior air suggested the aristocracy, but the style of their dress was foreign. The Old

Man had spent enough time bowing and scraping at Court to familiarize himself with the latest fashions, but these didn't look like anything he had seen in Italy or France. Likewise, he could feel the eyes of the occupants of the coach resting on him, and he worried that his clothing looked too obviously foreign.

The Old Man heard the laughter of children off to his right. He caught a few of their words and determined they were speaking in English. That would explain a few things, he thought to himself. He had never set foot on the British Isles, but had always heard about the strange manners and dress of the English.

"Hallo, hallo children," he called to them in his broken English.

"Who's that then?" one of them asked his playmates.

"Never seen him before," his friend responded quietly.

"Por favor—" He knew that was incorrect, but hoped that one of them might understand anyway. Instead they started backing away warily. This was not good. If they summoned their parents or the authorities, he might very well be snatched up. He patted his sides, looking for sweeties, and one hand found the soft paper book the two men had thrown from their carriage.

"Would one of you like this?" he asked in Italian.

The children didn't understand his words, but his meaning was clear. The tallest boy stepped carefully toward him, and when he was within reach, lunged forward and snatched the manual from his hand. He hurried back, but as soon as he discerned that no one was following him, turned around and eyed the Old Man curiously.

"He's an Eye-talian, he is," one of the others whispered.

"Naw, he ain't! He's French! Din't you hear him say 'poor favorie'?" said another.

"Excuse," the Old Man said to the tallest boy, and pointed toward the city ahead. He then raised his shoulders and turned his palms upward.

"You don't know where you're at?" asked the tall boy, feeling some measure of pride in deciphering his meaning. "That's London, that is!"

The Old Man's face lit up in recognition. He looked again at the city that sprawled before him and thought of the illustrations of London that he had seen. There was no mistaking the Tower of London ahead, but there were no walls or gates to the city. Could they have been overrun and torn to the ground in some massive recent battle? He would have to be on his guard.

"Merci," he replied.

"Any more questions?" the boy asked. "You got books, I got answers."

The Old Man hesitated briefly, and then shook his head no.

"You change your mind, just ask for me. I'm Sam Warner," said the boy.

"Sam Warner," repeated the Old Man, then reached out and shook hands with the boy. "Me—Leonardo DaVinci. Gratzie, mon frere."

And with that, the Old Man turned away and resumed his walk toward the city.

The children looked at each other. "Leonardo DaVinci? That's the man what painted all those pictures, ain't it?" asked one of them.

"Oh, he was havin' us on, that's all," said Warner.

"What you mean?" asked another.

"That bloke—the real one—he's been dead for hundreds of years," said Warner.

1848

Stan and Jack sifted through the wreckage of the NLE-13 at their feet. It had only been about ten feet off the ground when it crashed into the strange bat-winged woman, but the fall to the pavement below was enough to smash it to bits.

The timenauts fared much better than their craft. Aside from a few bruises, they were none the worse for wear as they climbed from the ruined craft.

"Whot the bloody 'ell you doin'?" screeched the bat-woman. "You damn near killed me!"

Upon closer inspection, they could see that the bat-winged creature was quite human—in fact, most attractive—save for the two large leather wings that appeared to be strapped onto her.

"Excuse us, but—can you actually fly with those things?" asked Jack.

"Not any more!" she fumed. "Are you blind? Where the devil did you come from, anyway?"

"We're not allowed to tell you," said Stan rather pointedly.

"Says who?"

"What my friend means," interrupted Jack, "is that we took a sharp turn without looking. It was all our fault. We're new here in..."

Jack's attempt to learn their location was meeting with a blank stare.

"...In any case..." muttered a defeated Jack.

"What year is this?" asked Stan.

The native stared at Jack, who gave her a reassuring look.

"Must have bumped his head when he fell," said Jack.

"Yeah," said the relieved native. "I was wonderin' 'bout 'im for a minute there."

This one wasn't giving out any information, the frustrated Jack thought to himself. This was the first time he had encountered this problem during a Time Hop. The NLE units were equipped with an infallible tracking device, in part to avoid these sort of embarrassing guessing games. Based on typical operation, Jack estimated that they had lost the NLE-13 Operator's Manual no more than fifty to one hundred years ago—a minor stroll down the hill for a couple of experienced timenauts like themselves. It was no big deal to hop back a century or so and retrieve a dropped booklet. The big deal would be their attempt to repair the time machine without the instruction book to guide them.

And there was still the question of the Old Man, who had suddenly appeared and just as quickly disappeared after they dropped the booklet. It had all happened too quickly for Jack to discuss it with Stan, but right now, Jack was leaning toward the opinion that the Old Man was simply an illusion, or at most a tiny burp in the Time Stream that they glimpsed when the booklet re-entered the Time Continuum. At least that was the simplest explanation, and so it would be the one Jack would cling to as long and as desperately as possible.

For the first time, Jack looked up at his surroundings and was relieved by what he saw. Though they had crash-landed in a small alleyway, at first glance there appeared to be no significant break with what he knew to be the historical record, aside from bat-winged aviators.

Then they stepped out into the courtyard and gazed at Piccadilly Circus.

The brightness of the lights dazzled them. These were not primitive torches or gaslights, but impossibly electric bulbs that shone in nearly every direction, blinking bulbs in every color urging passers-by to visit this restaurant or that ale-house. This miracle of the ages had been thoroughly co-opted by the advertising industry for their own crass, commercial purposes.

Jack's momentary disappointment was lessened when he looked skyward. Skyscrapers towered over them that should not have existed in Victorian England. The air was crisscrossed with more bat-winged fliers, and tracks for what appeared to be a streetcar in the sky hummed busily overhead.

The wind shifted slightly. The young woman with them (Jack decided it did her appearance a grave disservice to call her a bat-woman) apparently got a whiff of the dried manure that continued crumbling from Jack. She wrinkled her nose in disgust.

"Uh...you're okay, aren't you?" asked Jack cautiously. "I mean, you took a nasty spill there."

"Yeah, yeah, fine, fine," she responded.

"What year is this?" barked Jack.

"What do you mean?"

"I want to make sure you're okay," said Jack, trying to exude compassion without overdoing things. "What year is this? And what city are we in?"

"All right," she sighed, quickly tiring of the lunatics in front of him. "We're in London. And it's 1848. Now if you don't mind, I'll be going, and I'll thank you to look where you're goin' in the future."

The irony of her final words escaped both Stan and Jack as she walked off, dragging the pair of wings behind her like a defeated entrant at a Junior High Science Fair.

She was gone before they protest, and so Stan and Jack turned their attention to the Victorian marvels that surrounded them.

The pair watched the nearby hydraulic engine operating the elevator that rose at least 30 stories high. The success of such elevators undoubtedly led to the development of the skyscrapers that dotted the landscape of 1848 Britain. Of course, such a development also indicated an advancement in architecture and engineering.

If either of them had paid closer attention during their (required) history studies, they would have noticed thousands of impossibilities, as though a real-life "What's Wrong with This Picture" played out before their eyes. As it was, they spotted several of the most glaring. The canal that ran down the middle of the road didn't look right to either of them, nor did the one-man submarine emerging from the water.

Streetcars seemed to crisscross the entire city, connected to the electrical wires overhead like umbilical cords. There were indeed streetcar rails in the sky, a hundred feet up in the air, though not placed so closely together as to interfere with the air traffic.

But to them, the most glaring, conspicuous anomaly was in the center of the courtyard. It was a huge, bronze statue that towered over the people walking along beneath its gaze, and stood face-to-face with many of the people flying past in glider planes or on wings of leather.

Yet it wasn't the size of the imposing figure that towered over the courtyard that caught their attention, or the exquisite artistry of its design and sculpture, but its identity.

The timenauts stared at each other to be certain. Even though they had both gotten only the briefest of looks, there could be no mistake.

The face staring down at the 1848 Londoners was that of the Old Man. The one who had appeared out of nowhere and fallen from their Time Machine.

"It's him, all right," confirmed Stan. "Straggly beard, pointy nose—That's the guy that must have broken off the homing beacon when we lost the Instruction Manual. Wait till I get my hands on him—"

"What are you going to do? Knock him in a pile of dung, too?" Jack said derisively. "If that really is the same guy, this could be our lucky break."

"What do you mean?" asked Stan. "The real guy must be dead by now. He was about a hundred years old when he fell off Nellie, and that was at least fifty years back."

"I know that!" snapped Jack. "The point is, you dropped the Instruction Manual for Nellie the same time the Old Man fell, so they must have ended up in the same time. The Manual might still be around here. All we need to do is find it and use it to help us fix Nellie. Then we can go back and pick up the Old Man and the Operator's Manual right where we dropped them off. We'll have it all cleaned up. Neat and tidy."

It started to dawn on Stan.

"That's right! We could get out of this smelling like a rose!" he grinned, then caught himself. "But there's one thing that bothers me. What's the deal with all of these flying machines? And submarines? And skyscrapers? I don't think London was supposed to have canals in 1848."

"It still doesn't have canals, or any of this other Buck Rogers stuff!" exclaimed Jack, waving his hand. "What could have caused all this?"

"You don't suppose—the Old Man—?"

"One old geezer couldn't have caused all this," Jack said firmly.

"I wonder who the old guy was, anyway."

"I don't know, but I think we'd better find out," said Jack. "Let's take a closer look."

They wove their way through the bustling crowd. Like any big city, the passersby were careful to avoid eye contact, and the only attention given to the pair was due to the smell of manure. Jack had been virtually dipped in the stuff, and while Stan had grown accustomed to it, the 19th Century Brits had the good sense to avoid it as much as possible. In fact, the crowd seemed to part as Jack passed through it, making his way to the statue.

Standing at the base, the sculpted figure looked even more impressive. Even the birds in the courtyard—of which there were many—seemed to respect the Old Man, though the perches offered by his arms had apparently encouraged a few droppings on the street below. The inscription on the bronze plate on the base read:

Leonardo DaVinci
1452—1778
With the Thanks of a Grateful Nation
"Britannia Rules the World"

The odd nature of the message left Stan scratching his head.

"What's that supposed to mean?" asked Stan.

"It means our clean-up may not be as neat and tidy as we had hoped," muttered Jack.

"You mean we brought Leonardo DaVinci hundreds of years into the future?" Stan said, piecing it all together aloud.

"But—that could really mess up the time line. I mean, really bad!"

"I know."

"If he used 18th Century British technology to build his inventions, he could create—" said Stan.

"Submarines." noted Jack. "And flying machines. And canals, and lifts for skyscrapers, and—war machines?"

"Now wait a minute," cautioned Stan. "Let's not get carried away. I mean, the guy's dead now. He's been dead almost 75 years in this time line. How much damage could he possibly do?"

"How much damage has he already done?"

They both looked at the bronze plate once again, as Jack read the last line aloud.

"Britannia Rules the World..."

Chapter Six

The Near Future

The Chronological Apocalypse was rolling ever closer, but Franklin Hodges was taking the news remarkably well. Colonel Hall had just finished his de-briefing, and Hodges noticed with glee that the Colonel had referred to it as a "situation," once even slipping up and labeling it a "crisis." Good.

When the goddam military moved in and took over his entire operation, Hodges had fought it as vehemently as possible, knowing it was unlikely to do any good. And sure enough, all of their protests were in vain. All of his superiors were removed, leaving him in charge of a skeleton force. The first missions under the military—the "clean-up hops," as they were known—went all too smoothly, and Hodges had become rather perturbed. The better the military's operation looked, the worse it made his operation look.

When the clean-up operation was subjected to budget cuts, it only added insult to injury. Hodges sat back quietly as the finest, most gifted timenauts fled their organization for more lucrative opportunities in the private sector (in addition to, of course, writing books about their experiences—some bookstores were devoting entire sections to such spurious time-traveling memoirs). When the dust had settled, they were left with just two timenauts—Stan Keaton and Jack Wilson. Undoubtedly products of the old political patronage system, he had decided, each just barely competent enough to avoid being cut entirely. When they were down to one final mission, they were the last timenauts left standing and were chosen by default, after lengthy closed-door discussion. Of course, his own assessment of their abilities was ignored. The feeling among the military and appropriate members of the Senate Appropriations Committee was that since these two had the training and were on the payroll, they might as well use them, especially as the mission involved little more than a drive to the country to pick up a piece of litter.

And now this happened. Serves 'em right, the bastards. He had been waiting a long time for the military to fall flat on its face, and it now looked like his wait was over. The bombastic Colonel had spent the last half hour threatening, cajoling, even flattering him, but Hodges remained characteristically silent. The Colonel showed him the computerized readouts of the Time Anomaly headed their way, and it was huge.

Small ripples in the time pool were the norm, and everyone took them in stride. In fact, he had never seen anything bigger than a tiny undulating wave, and all of them had been repaired before coming close to doing any damage. But this—well, he could see why the Colonel and the military were so worried. This wasn't a tiny ripple, or even a wave. It was a tsunami. The goddam thing engulfed the screen and spilled out too widely to see any boundaries. It seemed limitless, and they were all scared shitless. *Well, you can't say I didn't warn you, Colonel!*

And now the military was planning to make him their whipping boy. That was the other bit of good news that Colonel Hall had dropped into his lap in a not-so-subtle way. Just as the military had completely screwed it all up, apparently beyond all redemption, they were going to drop it all back in his lap. Well, that was just delightful. They would make it look like it had all been his fault in the first place, and if he couldn't find a solution, it was going to be hung on his shoulders.

Yet when the Colonel gave him the news, he took it all good-naturedly.

Hodges knew the Colonel, despite being relatively cordial toward him on the outside, secretly hated his guts, but as the feeling was mutual, there were no particularly hard feelings. Little did he know, Hodges thought to himself. He had a plan for dealing with this new load of culpability. He knew precisely what he would do.

Nothing. Nothing at all. Not a damned thing.

Why should I? he thought to himself.

His options were perfectly clear. (1) He could help pull the Colonel's fat out of the fire and try to avert the chronological catastrophe. If he succeeded, the Colonel would undoubtedly end up blaming him and his crew for the whole debacle in the first place. (2) He could try to help and fail, and likewise take the blame. Or (3) he could refuse and walk away. Reality as everyone knew it would end (prior to which the Colonel would shift the blame to him), but he would have the opportunity to watch the Colonel spend his last days flailing about in panic. None of his accusations would matter once the time wave struck, anyway.

For Hodges, the choice was deliciously clear. Let the fat bastard sweat.

"I'm sorry, but I'm afraid there's really nothing more we can do on this end, Colonel," said Hodges with as much sincerity as he could manage.

Of course, it was true, but the enthusiasm Hodges had mustered up for the end of the world would have startled most people in any Time Line. He was barely able to conceal his delight from the Colonel.

"Nothing we can do—?" gasped the Colonel. "What the hell do you mean? This was your project! Your responsibility!"

"But Colonel, once you—the Army took control, you were operating outside our approved constraints—" protested Hodges with as much innocence as he could muster.

"Don't you try to blame this on the Army, you little turd!" barked the Colonel. "The Army didn't invent those goddam time machines of yours!"

"No sir, that's not what I meant," whimpered Hodges. "It's just that there isn't a tracking signal. We don't have any coordinates to work with. There's nothing we can do. It's like they just vanished completely out of time."

The Colonel was shaking with impotent rage.

"The Army does not just sit around doing nothing!" he bellowed. "The Army leads!"

"Yes sir! So what should we do first? " Hodges asked innocently.

"Um...ah..." stammered the Colonel.

Hodges tried not to smile. God, he was enjoying this.

"If you don't do something I'll have to take charge of this mission!" the Colonel barked.

Hodges tried to screw up his face as he responded "Sir, I thought you were already in charge of this."

"No! I mean, yes!" The Colonel was flummoxed. "Look, I didn't invent any goddam time machines! It's not my fault!"

"No, sir."

"Goddam right! Buck Rogers crap!" he spat.

"But when the Army took over the time machines, didn't they make you responsible? They must have thought you could handle it."

"Yes! No! Look, you were supposed to be monitoring this whole operation!"

"But sir, I can't have that sort of accountability without any responsibility, can I?" asked Hodges.

"Yes! No, you—" The Colonel stammered once last time, and then gave up. He stood up and walked to the door of the conference room, then pointed a finger menacingly at Hodges.

"Fix it! Or else!"

And with that, the Colonel stormed out of the room.

Hodges sighed and a great sense of calm enveloped him.

"Or else what?" He uttered softly to himself.

London 1768

Leonardo DaVinci sipped his wine slowly, savoring it as he had savored his years in London.

He shook his head. Had it really been seven years since he had arrived in the future? The time had just flown by. Once he had convinced Lord North that he was indeed The Great Leonardo DaVinci, the rest had all fallen into place.

Leonardo had spent a few days acclimating himself to 18th Century London upon his arrival. After kicking around the city for a couple of days, he had decided he was disappointed. Granted, there were a few advances in medicine, science and industry, but after 250 years, was this the best they could do? A true visionary could wrap this place around his little finger.

And so, he secreted himself away in his room at the Fox and Hound Inn for a few days, with pens, ink and rolls of blank parchment. He searched his memory for the inventions that would be sure to impress his intended audience, and started drawing, concentrating on those inventions with possible military applications. There was nothing nearer and dearer to a politician's heart than developing a new Weapon of Moderate Destruction, and Leonardo had plenty of those. Of course some of them, like the flying mechanism and the completely immersible vessel, had peacetime applications too, but that couldn't be avoided. He still had plenty of vicious, savage tools of death sure to warm the cockles of any ruler.

When he had drawn up a suitably impressive display of samples, he decided to seek out the movers and shakers of that era. A few carefully spent coins at the Fox and Hound soon loosened enough tongues to teach him the lay of the land.

King George III had been on the throne eight years now, and during the last three had been accruing a reputation for—well, eccentricity was the way one of his drinking mates had described it, though Leonardo knew exactly what he meant. What is eccentric in a King is often considered demented in someone without power or money. That didn't necessarily alter his plans—in fact, it might make them even easier to achieve.

His right-hand man was his Prime Minister, Lord Frederick North, an upper-class lackey whose toadying was a model for all of the aristocracy. Unfortunately, the Prime Minister expected to be the recipient of such similarly accomplished groveling from the citizenry, and heaven help anyone who failed to live up to his expectations.

With this forewarning, Leonardo presented himself at court as the emissary of an Italian nobleman, which was at least based on the truth. Of course, any Italian nobleman he might have represented would have been dead for over 200 years, but his subterfuge was successful enough to grant him an audience with Lord North and his military advisors.

The meeting had gone badly at first, until he presented them with his sketches and designs. By the time he felt brave enough to reveal his true identity, North and the others were so delightedly pouring over his plans for an armored tank that they barely paid him any mind. He had prepared an elaborate scenario for them, describing how he had taken a tumble in the Italian Alps, and was frozen solid for the past 250 years. He almost felt slighted when they ignored him to spend time looking over his documents.

King George was smitten with Leonardo's inventions, and soon, the Old Man himself. The dim monarch was enchanted with the story of his suspended animation, and soon had him doing sketches, asking him to reproduce some of his more celebrated paintings on parchment with pencils and charcoal. The King clapped excitedly after each one, and Leonardo was beginning to feel like a trained seal performing on command.

Looking back on it all, he was amazed at how easily he had been accepted into the Court. He could only attribute it to a combination of his brilliant inventions, their immediate applications for the military, and the fortuitous beginnings of dementia in the King himself. But whatever the reason, he had quickly become a Court favorite.

Science in the latter half of the 18th Century was actually more advanced than it had first appeared. Leonardo had studied the advances made by such luminaries as Sir Isaac Newton earlier that century, and applied those discoveries to his own research.

Leonardo took another sip of wine. He was dreading his next meeting, with the vulgar American Benjamin Franklin, who had been underfoot since before his arrival. Likewise considered a Court favorite by many, Leonardo found him to be an American apologist and an exceptionally tiresome whiner. Franklin had represented the American Colonies in London for several years now, and the Old Man simply didn't trust him. Franklin always had an axe to grind, and Leonardo knew that if he were not careful, it would wind up buried deep in his back. Franklin would be deep in the midst of his ribald stories, and before the laughter could die down, slip in a request to reconsider the latest tax on tea. He had actually appeared before the House of Commons not long ago and successfully argued for the repeal of the Stamp Act.

In his heart of hearts, Leonardo knew he was jealous of Franklin. The American was just as charming as Leonardo, yet without the talent to back it up. His greatest inventions couldn't hold a candle next to the lowliest creations of the great DaVinci. Spectacles? An improved stove—which he named after himself? And that wretched Almanack. How could people read such drivel and consider it clever?

Leonardo nearly snapped the stem of his wine glass thinking about him. The only area of interest in which the American even came close to him was in the study of electricity. Leonardo grudgingly admitted that Franklin had done some interesting research in that area, but had refused to divulge any significant findings. And whenever Leonardo tried to sit down with Franklin and wheedle anything out of him, the crass American would always insist on going out to public houses and whoring, the thought of which repulsed the refined Italian.

But today's meeting would be different. After talk of an American revolution had been firmly quashed thanks to DaVinci-designed weaponry, Franklin had been making nice-nice to all of the aristocracy. He had obviously decided upon which side his bread was buttered and was acting accordingly. But he had reckoned without the genius of the great DaVinci.

The Old Man drained his glass and poured himself another, emptying the bottle. He set it aside and reached into the crate below the table for another, making certain to select a cheaper, less desirable vintage to offer to his guest. His chambers were small but cozy. As Special Advisor to His Majesty King George III and de facto military advisor and chief science officer, Leonardo could have had his pick of offices, but preferred something less ostentatious, so as to give the commoners cause to admire his lack of pretension. Of course his laboratory was quite another story and, combined with his art studio, took up thousands of square feet nearby. But Leonardo preferred to foster this humble image, which had served him well up to this point.

He heard a minor commotion outside his door, and recognized an annoying voice spewing another "witticism." It was followed by laughter from Jameson, his manservant.

"Mr. Benjamin Franklin to see you, sir!" his servant called out from the foyer, still chuckling.

The Old Man summoned up his strength for the ordeal. Any one-on-one session with Franklin in which he was expected to be polite was always taxing on him.

Franklin stepped into his chambers, a beatific smile on his face. He hated that smile. Had the American gained weight? Buoyed by the thought, DaVinci returned his smile as Franklin waddled over toward his table and gave a polite, perfunctory bow.

"Signor DaVinci!" exclaimed Franklin. "How delightful to see you again!"

"And you, sir," he responded with feigned cordially, "Always a pleasure!"

DaVinci stood for a moment, nodded his head to acknowledge the bow, then sat again. With a sweep of his hand, he indicated for Franklin to take a seat.

"I hope I look as well as you do when I am 300 years old!" fawned the American.

"Little chance of that, Dr. Franklin!" he chuckled. "Very good of you to keep Jameson entertained."

"Just telling him the story of the Indian maiden and the traveling missionary—good man, that Jameson," said Franklin, and then lifted an eyebrow naughtily. "You, uh, have heard that story...?"

"Yes, yes, very amusing," DaVinci chuckled. He had heard no such story, but was anxious to cut Franklin off and frustrate him in the process.

"Let me pour you a glass of wine," DaVinci offered. "Or would you prefer some of your American whiskey?"

"Not before dinner, thank you," he replied. "Perhaps just the wine."

"Very good."

DaVinci reached for the bottle and began to remove the cork. Franklin saw the label, and recognized it for the pond water that it was, but before he could refuse, the cork was been removed and DaVinci was already pouring.

The Old Man saw the American's discomfort as he recognized the mediocre vintage.

"I hope this Chianti meets with your approval," he said innocently. "I know there are some who might barely consider it adequate, but you are like me. We are both ordinary man with ordinary tastes. There is nothing presumptuous about either of us, Dr. Franklin."

"N-no, no, I quite agree," said Franklin, taken aback for only a moment. There was no graceful way to protest the swill he was being given, so with no other choice, he accepted it gracefully, then held it to his nose. It had the distinct smell of vinegar.

"Something wrong, Dr. Franklin?" DaVinci asked innocently.

"No, no—although..." he said reticently.

"Yes?"

"It's just that I think this may have started to turn," said Franklin painfully.

"Ah, yes, you have a good nose," said DaVinci. "We are much alike, the two of us. We do not need a rare or exotic vintage! We are truly men of the people! A goblet with just a tinge of vinegar! That's what we like, isn't it, Doctor?"

"Uh, yes..."

"Nothing better for the bladder, either!" he smiled, hoping Franklin wouldn't notice his own glass already filled with expensive port. He raised it in the air, and Franklin joined him in the toast with somewhat less enthusiasm.

"I drink to us—to men of the people!" he said proudly.

Franklin touched his glass politely.

"Yes... To men of the people..." said Franklin.

Franklin managed a sickly smile as they each took a sip.

"Very—interesting..." managed Franklin.

"Oh yes. At our ages, we must look after our bladders!" said DaVinci, twisting the knife.

"Signor DaVinci, you know what an avid admirer I have always been of your works," said Franklin. "Your paintings are nothing short of magnificent! Your writings are brilliant, and your inventions—nothing short of genius!"

"Thank you," said DaVinci, not quite sure where this was all going. "Dr. Franklin is too kind. I am a great admirer of your work as well."

"You flatter me, Signor," smiled Franklin. "I am sure that two such humble talents as ourselves are capable of working out any problems that might ever arise between us."

Here it comes, thought the Old Man to himself as he smiled and nodded to Franklin.

"Apparently, His Majesty had some interest in studying my notes regarding my experimentation with electricity," explained Franklin, choosing his words slowly and carefully.

Ah yes, thought DaVinci, it was just as he had suspected.

"I was enormously flattered that our sovereign would find my own humble experiments worthy of his attention," said Franklin.

"Oh course—who wouldn't be?" asked the Old Man. Of course, the blue-blooded imbecile had no more interest in electricity than a fried egg; Franklin knew that as well as he did. Still, the Old Man admired—and was entertained by—his squirming. After all, the American couldn't come right out and accuse him of having his notes pilfered.

"Unfortunately, I was not in my residence when His Majesty sent his messengers to retrieve them for his own study," said Franklin.

There were a few moments of uncomfortable silence. The Old Man wasn't going to make this any easier for him than necessary. Finally, DaVinci gave a slight nod, as if to encourage him to continue. Franklin hesitated another moment, as if searching for the correct words before speaking again.

"And so...I wondered if...perhaps when His Majesty has finished perusing them...you might see your way clear to directing them all back to me?" said Franklin.

"Doctor Franklin, I had no idea His Majesty was so interested in your work with the kites. How flattering that must be for you! I am sure that your notes will be returned to you the moment he is finished with them," said DaVinci, who then lowered his voice and addressed the American more seriously. "After all, His Majesty is not a thief."

This appeared to rattle Franklin, just as he had hoped, and looked around quickly.

"Of course not, Signor! I would never make any such insinuation!" he replied.

Was that a tremble in his voice? This was such good sport!

"Do not worry, Dr. Franklin. Your words will go no further than this room," said DaVinci in a reassuring manner.

"No! That isn't what I meant!"

"Dr. Franklin, I am sure that losing these notes about your kite-flying experiments has found you to be over-wrought, and so I am sure I may overlook your accusations about His Majesty—"

"But Signor, I meant no accusations!"

"Still, I would suggest that you go back to your own chambers. After you rest for a while, surely you will see what folly your words are," said DaVinci. "I have no idea how you misplaced your notes. Perhaps I should speak with the Royal Physician—"

"No, no! Please, Signor! Do not tell anyone! I meant nothing!"

"Dr. Franklin, you know the King is not a common criminal. Leave and get some rest, and I will consider the entire matter forgotten."

The American was still protesting when Jameson escorted him away. Faithful Jameson had undoubtedly heard the juicy bits of their conversation, and within hours, everyone in the palace would know that Franklin had virtually called the King a burglar. He might be able to talk his way out of it—and he might not. Either way, it was of no consequence to the Old Man.

He walked over to his desk, turned a key in one of the drawers, and pulled out a journal. He sat down and turned the pages to Franklin's notes on electrical current.

Chapter Seven

London 1848

Victorian England had never looked so modern.

Everywhere they turned, Stan and Jack spotted an ominous, yet spectacular new inconsistency, from magnificent skyscrapers with electrical lifts, to smaller conveniences like a steam-powered nose hair clipper.

The city looked as though someone had randomly plucked technological breakthroughs from throughout the 19th and 20th Centuries, dropped them into a cocktail shaker containing traditional Victorian London sights, shaken, and then poured them all out once again.

Jack had traveled across Europe when he was younger and spent a few days in London, and he struggled to find his bearings. Most of the streets in the city grid were laid out in a familiar manner, though it was discomfiting to learn that a few of the major arteries had been replaced by canals. Guided by his dim remembrances, the pair made their way up one street and down another.

"What are we looking for again?" asked Stan, peering into open windows and doors as they walked.

"Anything that looks out of place," said Jack, who quickly caught himself. "Actually, strike that. Everything looks out of place."

"Where should we look?"

"Well, if somebody found the manual and figured out how to use it...that person—and the manual—probably wound up in the palace, or somewhere pretty important," reasoned Jack. "And if they didn't know how to use it...it probably got thrown out or burnt up or put away in a trunk somewhere."

"So where should we look?" repeated Stan.

"I don't know."

They stopped and looked around. There was an almost militaristic display of Union Jacks, in all shapes and sizes, lining the streets and alleyways. Jack looked closer. The bars extending from the center of the flags were bent at 90-degree angles.

"Maybe we should find out more about Leonardo DaVinci," suggested Stan. "If we knew where he came from, or where he was when he first arrived in this time period, maybe we could start looking in that area."

The pieces were all starting to fit together, thought Jack, and the picture was not pretty. "Britannia Rules the World." The militaristic display of flags and national symbols. And now this, the swastika-like Union Jacks.

There was nowhere near enough evidence to draw the conclusion he was dreading—after all, the swastika was a traditional Native American symbol. What were the chances that a fascistic government would adopt it a century before the Nazi Party? But still, something felt very wrong.

"Are you still here?" a familiar voice called out.

They turned to see the woman they had knocked out of the sky.

Her hostile, confused expression had been replaced by a genuinely puzzled glare. She was all the more attractive for it, thought Jack. During their earlier meeting, they had been too disoriented to pay much attention to her overall appearance. Under these calmer circumstances, Jack paused to take a closer look.

The woman was rather young, to be sure, but with an intelligent, worldly gleam in her green eyes that belied her youth. Long, mostly straight red hair cascaded down to her shoulders, which was (Jack couldn't help but notice) bringing out the green in her eyes. Her skin was light and creamy, with not a blemish on it.

She wore an attractive dark green dress, rather than her previous grey coveralls and bat wings. The dress revealed and concealed in all the right places, and might have even been considered bold for its time, though it was hard to judge with time so seriously out-of-whack. But no matter how well concealed, her shapely figure would have drawn attention in any era.

Stan was intimidated by beautiful women, especially those with a presence as powerful as the woman before them. "Um...yes..." he stammered.

Not wanting to give her the impression that Stan outranked him, Jack felt a need to speak up and establish his authority.

"We—we're still here," he faltered. "We—I mean, um... Your wings. Hey, where are your wings? I'm sorry—I hope we didn't ruin them."

"Well," paused the woman, taking the measure of the men before her. "No, not really. One of the support shafts needs to be braced, but I think they should be fine."

"We're really sorry," said Jack.

"Yeah," said Stan, "And when we saw you flying straight toward us—well, it took us by surprise. We're not used to that—"

"I know what you mean," nodded the woman. "You're foreigners. You're not used to seeing women in flying harnesses."

"Y-yes, that's right!" Jack stammered. "Of course, we see men in flying harnesses all the time—"

Stan gave him a puzzled look, but Jack stopped him with a cold stare before he could speak.

"I mean, men in flying harnesses are nothing new at all to us foreigners," Jack continued. "But women—well, that's a different story!"

"And so you think there's something wrong with women flying, just like men?" she asked sharply.

"Oh, heaven forbid!" said Jack. "Women can do anything men can do—and usually better."

Jack hoped he wasn't piling it on too heavily, but dammit, he had taken a liking to this girl and hoped she might reciprocate.

She eyed him with suspicion and proceeded to change the subject.

"So what did you do with your flying machine?" she asked.

"It's pretty much where we left it—well, where it crashed," Jack corrected himself.

"How did you get a Temporary Holding Permit so quickly?" she asked. Was that concern creeping into her voice?

"A Temporary—?" asked Jack.

"A Temporary Holding Permit—to leave it there?"

The uncomprehending look on their faces served as their answer.

"You mean you just—abandoned it right there?"

"I guess..." said Stan.

"If the Special Services finds it, you'll end up in Southwark for sure!" she said worriedly, lowering her voice and glancing around them.

"Southwark Prison?" asked a puzzled Stan.

"No, Southwark Cathedral," she said sarcastically. "Yes, of course Southwark Prison!" She literally threw up her hands. Against her better judgment, she seemed resigned to looking after the two of them.

"Follow me!" she ordered.

Stan and Jack tagged along, trailing their beautiful benefactor through the streets. As they hustled to keep up, they began to notice the faces in the crowd. Most seemed timid if not downright frightened, going about their business quickly and efficiently, with no wasted motions. They were especially leery of the well-dressed women and men. Many of the latter wore military-style uniforms, with armbands that featured the altered Union Jack. They were proud, confident, even arrogant, and the commoners stepped aside to make room for them.

Jack found it difficult to take the measure of their new ally. She was either at the lower end of the uppercrust, or the upper end of the lower crust. But, her willingness to help them appeared to place her on their side.

As they trekked back to the wreckage of Nellie, the pair also noticed a distinct lack of garbage in the streets. The cobblestones were literally shining. In strategic places all along the streets stood men with buckets, brooms, scrub brushes and pails of water. They were likewise dressed in costumes, though they were different from the military uniforms. The men stood at attention, constantly surveying every inch of the streets before them.

When a horse raised its tail across the square, a swarm of street cleaners descended on the offending waste, efficiently shoveling, cleaning and finally scrubbing the spot clean. They then calmly picked up their cleaning tools and went back to eyeing the street from their respective places. The man on the horse—obviously a high-ranking soldier or aristocrat—paid no attention and rode off the moment his horse had done its business. He didn't seem worried about any Temporary Holding Permit.

The incident called attention to another peculiarity. It was Victorian London, yet that was the first horse they had seen on the streets. Could the electric streetcars have taken such a hold on the population?

Nellie was just as they had left her. Passersby seemed to take an extra step away from her, apparently so as not to be associated with this ugly, apparently illegal pile of rubble. Jack figured they were lucky to have crashed in this out-of-the-way alley, so as not to attract the attention of the uniformed types.

"Should we move it out of the way until we can fix it?" asked Jack.

"You're going to try to fix this pile of scrap metal?" asked the woman.

"We don't have much choice," Stan pointed out. "If we don't, we'll be stuck here forever."

"What my friend means to say," Jack interjected, "is that we need to take it someplace where we can store and try to repair it."

"There's a place just up the road from my house," she offered. "They're very good at fixing flying machines."

"That's not exactly what we need," explained Jack. "This is a special flying machine."

"Doesn't look so special to me," she sniffed, "apart from it being in a thousand pieces."

"No, no, this is—an experimental machine," said Jack. "We're going to have to repair it ourselves."

"Yeah, except we lost the Operator's Manual around here somewhere, so we have to find that before we can patch it up," said Stan.

"What happened to the wings?" she asked, studying the wreckage.

"Uh—that's right!" said Jack. "There's no wings! That's why it's so special!"

"I see," she said. "So it must have spinning blades on top, like one of those whirligigs I heard about. Where do you come from, anyway?"

"We're from the Corporate States—the United States of America," said Jack.

"What?" she asked curiously. "That's the first time I've heard of anybody calling it that. You don't mean the Colonies, do you?"

"Right," said Jack slowly. "The American Colonies...of Britain. That's what we call it over there. Right?"

"That's where we're from," noted Stan. "We can't go back until we get Nellie—"

"That's our flying machine—"

"Yeah, Nellie is a nickname," said Stan. "It's really called the NLE-13. That's how we got here."

"You mean to say you flew all the way from the Colonies in this new flying machine?" queried the disbelieving woman.

"That's right," said Stan.

"That's impossible," said the woman.

"Oh yeah? You don't believe us? Well, that's not all—" started Stan.

"Wait a minute!" interrupted Jack. "Look, Miss...uh..."

The woman paused for a moment to consider whether to reveal her identity to these two possibly deranged foreigners. Stan's guileless eyes and Jack's warm smile won out against her better judgment.

"Maggie," she said. "Maggie Wells. And you are—?"

Stan and Jack introduced themselves politely.

"But remember, Nellie is a big secret!" said Stan. "We'll get in big trouble if anybody finds out—"

"Are you sure you two don't work for Special Services?" asked Maggie.

"What's that?" asked Stan innocently.

"Are you trying to tell me you don't know—" Maggie looked around cautiously and lowered her voice. "—You don't know about Special Services?"

"Uh...no?" asked Jack.

"Either you two are lying, or you just got here—and you fell on your heads," she said, looking at Stan. "But for some reason, I feel like I can believe you."

"Thank you!" said a relieved Stan.

"What's all this about Special Services?" asked Jack, lowering his voice. "Are those the people walking around with the twisted armbands?"

"Where have you two been for the last hundred years?" she asked.

"Believe me, you don't want to know," replied Stan.

"The people with the armbands aren't the ones you have to worry about," she confided. "It's the ones that don't wear armbands that are the worst. They're the Queen's spies— they're judge, jury and executioner in one nasty package. That's how I know you're okay. If you would've been SpecServ, you would have killed me right after we collided."

"Nice people," said Jack.

"The only thing I don't understand is if you're not SpecServe, who are you? And how did you get a flying machine like this?" she asked.

"Do you have someplace we can take this?" asked Jack. He was getting increasingly uncomfortable talking to her in the open alleyway.

"Well..." she considered. "We could carry it to the stable behind my house. My mother'll be taking her nap about now, so maybe we could get it there before she wakes up. If anybody sees us, we'll just tell 'em it's another flying machine. They won't think nothin' of it. It's not the first time I brought home a flying machine."

No, Jack thought to himself as they reached down to pick it up. *But is it the first time you've brought home a pilot?*

Chapter Eight

The Near Future

Corporal Frank Spumoni was starting to grow concerned. He had never seen so much brass in one place. The monitoring station was no bigger than his uncle's greasy spoon back in Iowa, but he had never seen his uncle's cafe this crowded. There were officers and politicians everywhere, conversing quietly in small clusters and occasionally addressing the entire group. He was hearing things he probably had no business hearing—he was certain he didn't have the proper clearance for much of it—but everyone either forgot he was there or simply ignored him.

The only person in the room who didn't look concerned was Mr. Hodges. He sat with a lackadaisical expression, thumbing through the old issues of Golf Digest that were lying around the station. Occasionally, one of the generals or the suits would chew out Colonel Hall and Mr. Hodges would look on, lifting his eyebrows with an expression that said, "I told you so."

It had been going on like this for the past twelve hours. It began shortly after he made his first phone call to report the situation, and Frank was starting to get a little tired of all the excitement. It was cutting into his putting.

Suddenly, one of the men in suits wheeled around and sharply, accusingly singled out Mr. Hodges.

"Why isn't there a back-up tracking device?" he barked.

Hodges looked a bit startled, but recovered quickly.

"I recommended that, sir, but I was overruled," he said quietly. "I was told there were budgetary concerns."

His accuser turned back to face Colonel Hall.

"Satisfied, Colonel?" he asked. "See what happens when you try to save a few pennies? This is gonna cost us a goddam fortune!"

Another of the men in suits, one with a clearer grasp of the situation, pointed out that it was no longer a question of spending money, but of the sheer impossibility of their entire situation.

"If we could install another tracker on the NLE-13 right now, we wouldn't need to," he pointed out, though he was met by uncomprehending stares.

"Of course we need to!" growled a General. "It's a goddam public relations nightmare! We better look like we're doing something!"

"Well sir," another of the suits said calmly, as though he were explaining the matter to a schoolboy. "If we could find the Time Machine—wherever it is in the past—then we wouldn't need to install a tracking device to let us know where it is."

Blank stares.

"Because we'd already know!" he implored them.

The officers looked at each other. More blank stares.

"Sounds like a load of crap to me!" muttered one.

"Nevertheless, Colonel, it is crap for which you and your people are responsible," accused a suit.

Tempers began to flare. After a few more accusatory remarks and insinuations, it became clear that nothing more could be done. It was a testament to the clear-headedness of both groups that they stumbled upon the time-honored strategy for dealing with such situations: they began casting about for someone else to blame.

"Communists" were quickly ruled out, as were "Terrorists," "Right-wing Fundamentalists," "Left-wing Nutjobs," "Enviro-Avengers," "Survivalists" and "Neo-Nazis."

There was a momentary silence. Corporal Spumoni held his breath. There was no way they could pin this on him. Was there?

Suddenly, the Colonel heard a rustling of paper, and turned to see Mr. Hodges studying photos of a new plush new golf course just outside Yokohoma. He was oblivious to the conversation going on around him, intent on someday playing the 15th Hole, the one with peacocks on the island in the middle of the water hazard. Hodges looked up from the magazine to see over a dozen pairs of eyes studying him.

"Of course, it really all started with the eggheads," the Colonel said.

"That's right," said a General with a white moustache. "If they hadn't invented this thing in the first place..."

"They must have known what would happen," said one of the suits, shaking his head. "But they went ahead and built it anyway."

"And now look at the mess we're in," said the Colonel. "Well, they got us into this, so they can just get us out!"

"That's right," another one of the suits asserted. "This will ultimately fall under the jurisdiction of the scientists."

The unanimous shaking of heads struck fear in the heart of Mr. Hodges. "B-but we were taken off the project!" he protested. "There were no problems when we still had jurisdiction!"

"Come on, Hodges!" barked a Major General. "Be big enough to take responsibility for your own invention!"

This was precisely what Hodges had hoped to avoid.

"You can't get away with this!" warned Hodges. "Everybody knows the military took charge of all this. You can point your finger at me, but everybody's still going to be blaming you!"

The men in suits seemed to step back and consider this, and slowly eyed the military.

"You're goddam nuts!" said a Colonel, not used to being addressed in that tone. "I think we've got a Section 8 here, General."

The General lowered his voice. "He's not in the Army."

"So we can't court martial him..." noted another obviously disappointed Colonel.

"The man has a point," said the first suit. "Looks like the military has to get the blame for this one."

"That's a load of crap!" snapped yet another General, who then pointed at Hodges. "It's him, and those other candy-assed scientists!"

Several of the officers began speaking at once, and the suits started to reply. Not sure whether to say anything, Hodges sat and watched them square off. What could he do to cover his own ass—if anything? And then the glimmer of an idea suddenly sparked in his brain.

The scene was growing uglier, and the calm, measured tones had long since escalated to angry shouts. But just as the cacophony began to peak, the next alarm sounded.

All activity in the room suddenly came to a halt, and the room was silent except for the steady *beep-beep-beep* of the alarm. They turned to Corporal Spumoni, uncertain of its meaning but knowing it was probably bad news. He shifted uncomfortably in his seat, then sat up and leaned over the control board. He studied the rows of buttons and lights, feeling their gaze on him and knowing they expected him to have the answers. There was a blinking red light in the upper right hand corner of the keyboard that seemed suspicious. He glanced out of the corner of his eye to make sure they were still watching him, and moved his finger to the button beneath it. Then he noticed Hodges watching him as well. He gave a slight, almost imperceptible shake of his head, and Corporal Spumoni immediately removed his finger, just before he nearly deleted most of the information involving the crisis.

"I—I'm really not sure about this one," admitted Corporal Spumoni.

"What are you talking about, soldier?" asked an indignant General. "You're trying to tell us you don't know why that goddam thing is beeping? What the hell are we paying you for, anyway?"

"Well sir, all I was supposed to do was call you when the alarm went off. And that's what I did. Mr. Hodges is the only one who knows how the time machines really work."

"See? It's the damned eggheads!" snapped the Colonel. "I knew it!"

"All right then, Hodges," growled the oldest General. "If you know anything about the alarm, this would be a good time to tell us!"

Hodges raised an eyebrow. Talk about your instant karma, he thought to himself.

"I'm sorry, sir, but us 'candy-assed scientists' don't respond so well when we're threatened," he said quietly. "That's what happens when someone tries to turn us into scapegoats."

"You little—" muttered the Colonel. His face sank in defeat, and his demeanor slowly changed with that realization.

"So, Hodges, looks like you've got us over a barrel," grumbled one of the suits.

"Tell us why that alarm's going off, and we'll hang it on— well, we won't hang it on you," said another of the suits.

Several of the Officers glanced at him sharply. It appeared one of them would say something, but they nevertheless remained silent.

"All right then," said Hodges cautiously. "Let me have a look."

Corporal Spumoni moved away from the console, and Hodges took his place behind the control board. He pressed two keys, and the annoying *beep-beep-beep* stopped, but he continued to look at the closest screen. A series of colorful, pulsating rings emanated from the center. Hodges' brow was furrowed as he studied the screen.

"Is that it?" asked the oldest General. "Is the—problem solved?"

"What happened?" asked a suit. "What set it off?"

"No, no, I don't know, and I don't know," said Hodges.

"You trying to be funny?" growled the oldest General.

"No sir," said Hodges. "Just answering your questions."

Hodges took one last look at the monitor, pushed himself away from the console with both hands, then stood up and slowly turned to face the group eyeing him uncertainly.

"If our only problem was the alarm—then yes, it's solved," he said. One of the more dim-witted officers appeared to sigh in relief, but straightened up immediately when a sidelong look at his fellows showed no such similar relief. He furrowed his brows alongside them.

"Unfortunately, according to the monitor, it looks like the Chronological Apocalypse has reached the year 1860 and is rapidly heading this way," explained Hodges.

"That sounds like bullshit to me!" croaked the Colonel. "How do we know you're not making this up?"

"Could I have a piece of paper?" Hodges asked the group.

One of the suits tore a piece of lined yellow paper from his note pad, and then handed it to him. Then Hodges gave the Colonel a pen and the piece of paper.

"Okay, who was the president in 1861, just at the start of the Civil War?" he asked the group.

The politicians and the officers looked at each other warily.

"That would be Abraham Lincoln," one of them offered tentatively. The others began nodding slowly, fearing a trick.

"Okay, Colonel, write 'The American president in 1861 was Abraham Lincoln,'" said Hodges.

The Colonel reluctantly complied.

"Now hold that paper," said Hodges. "You shouldn't have to hold it for long, I'm afraid."

"What the hell's this all about, Hodges?" asked the oldest General.

"Well, General, I'll try to explain," said Hodges. "Who was the first president of the United States?"

The group looked at each other blankly, as though the question itself was incomprehensible. He might just as well have asked them what the universe looked like a half hour before the Big Bang.

"The first President?" one of the suits asked.

"That's right," said Hodges, encouraging them. "Lincoln was the sixteenth president, wasn't he?"

Several of the group nodded, feeling sure of themselves.

"So who was the first?" he asked them.

Blank stares.

"I don't know..." a General stammered.

"Shouldn't we know that?" asked another General.

"Are you sure it wasn't Lincoln?" asked a voice from the back of the room.

"What year did America win its independence from Britain?" countered Hodges.

"Independence?" asked another suit. "But we're a Colony—I mean, we were a Colony. Right?"

"All right, then let's try something else," said Hodges. "When was the first solo transatlantic flight?"

"Finally an easy one!" smiled the Colonel. "May 1858, with Roger Coopersmith flying for the British Empire."

He looked around to see the others smiling confidently with him.

"Okay then Colonel," said Hodges slowly, "Who was Charles Lindbergh?"

"Easy!" beamed the Colonel. "First solo transatlantic flight, 1928, the Spirit of Saint—"

The Colonel caught himself and stopped short as the implications of his answers grabbed him by the balls. The others looked equally startled. The Colonel grabbed a file cabinet to steady himself as his mind reeled.

"What the hell is this?" he stammered. "Coopersmith—Lindbergh—they didn't both do it first! What's going on here, Hodges? Am I cracking up?"

Hodges had finally gotten their undivided attention and planned to make the most of it. He began speaking as he would speak to a class of remedial learners: loudly and slowly.

"You see, something began going wrong in the late fifteenth or early sixteenth century," said Hodges. "There was a minor anomaly, though we don't think it had much affect on the Time Line. However, in the mid-eighteenth century, things apparently started to deconstruct at a rapid rate. That's where the anomaly became dangerous, completely destroying all vestiges of the Time Line, where it started re-assembling itself in a very—dissimilar manner. Instead of following along its prescribed path, this anomaly was so large and disruptive that as it continues toward the present day, it will wreak havoc on everything—and everyone—around us.

"Right now, that anomaly has reached the 1860s. Everything that has happened from the late fifteenth century up until the 1860s has been completely changed, but because those changes aren't finalized, they haven't completely settled in our brains. We remember a few of the more momentous events, but time is weaving itself a new pattern, and it's gotten as far as the 1860s. Everything that has happened since then is still the same—for now, but it's being rapidly displaced by this Anomaly Creep headed our way. Right now, we remember two different histories—the last century and a half, and the earlier centuries—and they don't always mesh together. That's why you remember two people being the first to fly solo across the Atlantic, except they were in different centuries. They don't match up, they haven't knitted themselves together—and they never will. Instead, the earlier version is going to replace everyone and everything today as it creeps along, wiping out everything in our Time Line—including us."

The room was completely silent. Hodges didn't know whether he had succeeded in describing their situation until one of the Generals in the back timidly raised his hand.

"Isn't there anything we can do?" he asked.

"Are you sure about this?" asked another.

"Yeah, how do we know this isn't all bullshit?" asked the Colonel.

Hodges glanced at his watch, then walked over to the screen. He studied it silently for a moment, and then turned to the Colonel.

"Colonel, who was president of the United States in 1861?" asked Hodges.

The Colonel concentrated for a moment.

"There—there wasn't a president in 1861," he finally said. "We were still a British colony. The Fultons were still leading commando raids against the Crown."

Several other heads nodded in agreement.

"Would you read what you wrote on that paper a few minutes ago?" asked Hodges.

The Colonel held it in front of him.

"'The American president in 1861 was Abraham Lincoln,'" he read, and then gasped at its apparent impossibility. "But—but—that's not right! I don't think he became president until 1862—or was it 1863? I mean, I know I just wrote it a couple of minutes ago—and it is my handwriting—"

Hodges surveyed the puzzled looks. "The Chronological Anomaly—the Time Wave—has, from our perspective, just caught up to the year 1861 and washed over it. Right now, as we look into the past, Abraham Lincoln was the American president in 1862, but he doesn't even exist before that. In fact, he was never even born."

"Do you remember ever hearing anything about Lincoln before 1862?" asked Hodges.

Mouths opened and jaws dropped, but no recognizable words emerged from any of them.

"And pretty soon, the Time Wave will have washed past 1865, and Lincoln will never have existed at all," said Hodges. "None of you will recognize the name of Abraham Lincoln."

The officers and government agents looked around the room. They were hoping—praying—that they could dismiss Hodges as some sort of lunatic and go home, but something about his explanation seemed too true to deny, especially with Colonel Hall's paper before them.

"So what are we going to do about this?" asked the oldest General.

"Do? I'll tell you what we're going to do," harrumphed another General. "We're going to send another one of these time travelers back there to straighten everything out! But a soldier, this time, by God! We'll get the job done right! Strap a 20mm missile launcher onto him, and we can take care of any Chronological Animorphing!"

"Remember when the government cut off funding for the whole project? And all of the Time Hoppers that hadn't fallen apart were dismantled?" asked Hodges.

"Do you have a point here, Hodges?" asked the Colonel.

"My point is that even if we wanted to send somebody off into the past, we couldn't do it because there aren't any more Time Hoppers! And there's nowhere near time to build one before the Time Wave wipes us all out!" said the increasingly frustrated Hodges.

"That's negative thinking, soldier!" barked another General.

"I'm not one of your goddam soldiers!" snapped Hodges.

"There's your real problem, Colonel," said the General. "Civilians."

"No, the real problem is that you people won't get your heads out of your asses long enough to listen to me!" said Hodges, in what was turning into a rant. "We had this whole program under control—more or less—and then the military and the politicians came in and took over. You threw out most of the people who knew anything about it, and started making up a bunch of asinine rules. And now you've screwed it up so bad that you've got a Time Wave headed right this way, about to wipe out our entire reality, and all you can worry about is 'How can we blame this on the scientists?' Let me tell you bozos something—it doesn't matter WHO you blame it on, because in less than three days, that Time Wave is going to hit, and there's NOTHING any of us can do about it! NONE of us are going to be around, because we'll have never existed in the first place!"

There was momentary silence in the room, and one of the suits leaned toward the oldest General.

"General Dunavan," said the suit, "I think we'll need to schedule a meeting about this whole thing, and the sooner, the better. How does next Thursday look?"

"What the hell are you people thinking?" erupted Hodges. He heaved a sigh, threw down his hands in disgust and shook his head. "That's too late! It's already too late! Don't you people GET IT?"

He stared at the uncomprehending faces before him, then turned and stormed out of the room. The men remaining in the room relaxed visibly, and the oldest General turned back to the suit.

"Next Thursday around three o'clock works for me," replied General Dunavan.

Chapter Nine

London 1848

Stan and Jack managed to pick up most of the rubble where Nellie had plummeted to the ground. There were stabilizer and energizer components strewn at least twenty feet in each direction, but they grabbed everything they could see and stuffed them in their pockets. They both sighed with relief when they spotted the principal gyrogear and the mainline power crystal. Maggie offered up a burlap bag for some of the larger pieces, but the seats, the mainframe and the remaining large parts would have to be carried as they were.

Though Stan and Jack were nervous at first, it didn't matter in the end. None of the passersby gave them a second glance as their junkyard caravan marched through the streets as unobtrusively as possible. At one point, when they stopped to re-arrange their load, a uniformed official with an armband called from down the block. "Get that junk off the street as quickly as possible!" They shouted a polite, suitably deferential "Yes sir!" and he never looked back.

They turned into an alley and found themselves at the stable.

"We don't have a horse anymore, but we still have a couple of stalls here," explained Maggie. "We keep our horseless carriage in one of them."

When Jack asked if that was common, Maggie explained that most folks who could afford it had done the same, and the only people who still used horses were the underclasses and the military. The latter used them for parades and drilling, as all of their actual battles utilized the most up-to-date war machinery.

Before she could go into more detail, an older, balding man approached.

"Afternoon, Miss Maggie," he greeted her cordially. "Nice day for a bit of flying."

He snickered in a polite yet condescending *isn't it ridiculous that a woman nowadays wants to have anything to do with that darned fool flying business* manner. Maggie had long since learned to ignore him.

"Wally, this is Stan and Jack," she said. "And this is Wally."

"Nice to meet you fellas," said Wally with a knowing look—though whatever he may have thought he knew couldn't possible have been close.

"Our pleasure," said Jack.

"Nice place you have here," said Stan sincerely.

"Thanks," said Wally. "You from the Colonies then?"

"Uh—yeah, yeah," said Jack. "Miss Wells is allowing us to store our flying machine here until we can repair it."

Stan and Jack began emptying their pockets and piling the pieces next to Maggie's bag, which was leaning next to the back wall in one of the stalls. They placed the mainframe in the center of the stall, planning to cover it with an old blanket.

"You young'uns and your flying machines," Wally chuckled to himself. "If the good Lord woulda wanted us to fly—"

"He'd have given us wings?" interrupted Maggie. "But he didn't, did he?"

"Nope, you got yours from James Burton," said Wally.

Maggie appeared uncomfortable at the mention of his name.

"Yes, yes, we've been through all this before, Wally," she said. "But you're not talking me out of flying."

"Suit y'self," smiled Wally. "You want me t'have a look?"

"No, no!" said Jack, too quickly to be polite. Fortunately, Wally hadn't noticed.

"I been tinkerin' with some of those horseless carriages," offered Wally. "Reckon they can't be too different from these here flyin' machines."

"You'd be surprised," said Stan. "It's—"

"It's—an experimental model," said Jack quickly.

"Now Wally, be sure to take care of this thing," said Maggie. "We'll be stoppin' back soon to get it running again."

The three of them left Nellie in the sometimes-capable hands of Wally and Maggie led them to her house.

"Wally worked for my father before he passed on," she explained. "You can trust him."

"Who's James Burton?" asked Jack.

"He gave me—he's just someone who is interested in flying machines," she replied. "He had an extra pair of wings, and he knew how much I—he gave them to me."

"Even a pair of wings must cost a lot nowadays, don't they?" asked Jack.

"Yes—well, not for somebody like James," she said. "He is rather well-off."

"Are you—keeping company with him?" asked Jack tentatively.

"Oh, he's just a friend," she replied.

Jack thought she looked slightly uncomfortable, and figured there must be a much longer story behind it all. Just his luck. Granted, Maggie was technically old enough to be his great-great-great-great-great-great-grandmother. The rules against that sort of fraternizing with natives outside their own eras were—well, he could be locked up for the rest of his life if he were caught. Not worth taking a chance on, but at the moment, certainly fun to fantasize about. Maggie was not at all what he had been expecting in women of that era. She was educated, confident, and unafraid to speak her mind—she could teach the women of the future a thing or two. And she was very easy on the eyes, as well. Fun to fantasize about, indeed.

The stable was a short distance from Maggie Wells's home, where she lived with her widowed mother. The two-story home was in the center of the block, surrounded by other once-proud structures that were now all falling into disrepair.

Maggie invited Stan and Jack inside, where Mrs. Wells was indeed napping. It was also the housekeeper's day off, she explained; even though the family was not as well-off as they had once been, old Mrs. Hartigan still lived with Maggie and her mother and did the cooking and the cleaning. After more than twenty years, Mrs. Hartigan was like family.

The shapely redhead went to the kitchen and emerged with half a loaf of bread and a slab of cheese, along with a freshly uncorked bottle of wine. It had been a while since they had last eaten, and Stan and Jack needed little encouragement to dig in.

"My mother never lets anyone walk away from here hungry," she said. "I'm sorry we don't have anything more. We can't really afford a freezing machine."

"A what?" asked Stan between mouthfuls.

"Those new electrical freezing machines," she explained. "They're all the rage with the aristocracy. They store meat and other perishable food. Haven't you heard of them?"

"Oh, of course," said Jack, suddenly comprehending and glaring at Stan, who was slicing another piece of bread.

"Now Miss Wells, we're going—" said Stan.

"Maggie," she corrected him, and Jack smiled at her.

"Okay, Miss Maggie, we're going to have to start working on Nellie as soon as possible," said Stan.

"Well, I'll be happy to give you a hand," she offered. "Wally, too, though he isn't quite as mechanically inclined as I am."

"Actually, the situation is a little more—complicated than that," explained Jack. "The Operator's Manual has the instructions that we need to put Nellie back together. The only problem is, we can't find the Operator's Manual."

"What does it look like?" she asked.

Jack described the booklet and the cover design, but she shook her head no.

"When did you lose it?"

"Just before we—actually, I'm not sure. A long time ago. Years ago…" Jack caught himself.

"Where did you lose it?"

"Well, we're not sure of that either," admitted Stan.

"It should be somewhere around here…I think…" said Jack.

"Well, that narrows it down," she said, rolling her eyes. "You need your book to get back home. But, you don't know where you lost it, and you don't know when you lost it. Sorry, gents, but it sounds like you're not going home for a long time."

Scotland 1788

Benjamin Franklin used a small stick to stir up the ashes in his fireplace. The fire had nearly gone out while he napped, and now he was trying to coax it back to life. His tiny cottage, the only one on the small island off the coast of Scotland, got cold in the wintertime, much too cold for his elderly bones. Firewood had to be conserved.

"Dr. Franklin?" called a voice from outside. Eric, his even more elderly servant and the only other occupant of the island, sounded agitated.

"What is it?" he moaned.

Franklin had just woken. The sparse grey hair on his left side was sticking out perpendicular to his head, while the hair on the right was flat against his head. He halfhearted attempted to make them symmetrical with his fingers, but with no one else on the island but Eric, he felt no urgent need for grooming.

Just outside the door stood Eric and three mysterious figures, tightly clutching blankets and heavy wraps.

"He's awake," Eric said to the three strangers. "This is the man you'll be wanting to talk with, and I daresay, he'll appreciate the company. Not that he and I don't get along just swell, mind you, but sometimes he gets tired of talking to just me, because I'm the only one he's had to talk to for more than a month now, and even though I do more than my part to keep the conversation fresh, there's only so much one fella can do, to be blunt, and he's gotten more crotchety as he's gotten older, not as much fun to be around if you know what I—"

"What is it, Eric?" snapped Franklin from inside. He thought he heard Eric rattling on, which would not be surprising; there didn't seem to be two minutes that went by without Eric rambling on, whether or not there was anyone around to listen. Franklin was convinced the man couldn't breath unless his vocal cords were in constant motion. He suspected an autopsy on Eric would reveal much, and he hoped to be the one to perform it. And sooner, rather than later.

"Of course, he's not supposed to have any company, officially, of course, but I doubt if anybody would care, even if they noticed," said Eric to the three, then called inside: "Visitors!"

Franklin gave a start, and then stumbled to his feet, now fully alert.

"Well, come in!" he called, "You'll catch your deaths out there!"

Eric pulled the door open, and Franklin saw three cloaked figures standing before him.

"You must be frozen!" he said as he motioned them to enter. "Come in. May I offer you a cup of tea?"

The three of them entered, followed by Eric, who slammed the door shut against the north wind. Two men and a woman threw off their cloaks. When he got a look at the woman, an attractive redhead, Franklin quickly tried to fix his hair.

"Thank you for meeting with us, Mr. Franklin," said the taller of the two men.

An American, he noted to himself; obviously not an emissary of His Majesty, and highly unlikely to be conveying a pardon. Oh, well, right now he was simply grateful for the company of anyone who wasn't Eric.

"It is my pleasure," he bowed to them, smiling. "Please pardon the clutter, but I find I am not used to receiving visitors this time of year. Eric, could you get us all a cup of tea?"

"We don't want to be any trouble," said the woman in an obvious British accent.

"No trouble at all!" said Franklin, winking at the young woman.

"Oh, please permit me to introduce myself," she said. "I am Maggie Wells, and my friends are Stan and Jack."

They each took a step closer and shook hands.

"It is my great pleasure to welcome all of you," said Franklin.

"The pleasure is ours, sir!" said the shorter man, also an American.

"Any friends of Maggie Wells are friends of mine!" cracked Franklin. "Now then, what can I do for you?"

"Well, actually sir," said Jack, "We'd like you to see if you could share some of your electrical know-how with us."

"Me?" he smiled, though he showed a hint of surprise. "I'm not much of an expert on electricity nowadays. His Majesty has—taken charge of such matters."

"We have the ultimate faith in your abilities," said Maggie. "And we do have one other request. Could you take us to your good friend Leonardo DaVinci?"

"Actually, Signor DaVinci and I have not spoken..." Franklin began, and then caught himself suddenly. "DaVinci? Leonardo DaVinci? But—but Signor DaVinci has been dead for years!"

"We realize that, Dr. Franklin," said Maggie. "But we're hoping that won't be a problem."

Chapter Ten

London 1848

Sam Warner pulled out the battered black trunk from the cubbyhole below the staircase.

"I'm cleaning it out right now!" he called to his wife Sarah in the next room. "Will that make you happy?"

His very pregnant wife heaved a sigh.

"I told you Sam, we have to make room with another baby on the way, and you can't keep all of your old junk!" she lectured.

"A baby on the way" was an overused excuse in the Warner household, but Sam knew it was pointless to argue. It had most recently been invoked to purchase and move into a flat not far from where he had grown up. With this, their ninth baby on the way, Sarah had been increasingly anxious to "fix up the house."

Nesting instinct, Sam supposed. That was fine with him, but it had already started cutting into his work schedule. As one of London's most promising young inventors (which is what he considered himself), Sam didn't have much concern for spring cleaning, but decided to humor her.

"Junk?" he asked. "These are meaningful keepsakes from my childhood."

"Sam Warner, you've never opened that thing in all the years I've known you," she said, and waddled over to the trunk. "Let's see what you keep in there that's so important!"

She deftly undid the latches, and as the hinges squeaked, she pulled the lid open. Looking inside, she shook her head at the worthless junk her husband had been saving for years. There were bits of string, a few lead soldiers, and some old clothing.

"There, see?" said Sam anxiously. "Perfectly good clothing for the baby!"

"Good clothing?" she asked sharply. "These things are twenty years old!"

To illustrate her point, she picked up one of them and held it out to the defensive Sam.

"Look at this! Not only is it dirty—it looks like something you probably wore when you were a baby—"

As she spoke, a book fell from one of the folds in the material onto the floor in front of them.

"What's this?" she asked.

She picked it up and read "*NLE-13 Operator's Manual.*"

Sam stared at it with wide eyes.

"Well, look at that! I haven't seen that since—I don't remember when!" he gasped, then reached over and grabbed it.

"What is it?" she asked.

Sam paged through it, glancing at the cryptic drawings and confusing language.

"I'm not sure," he answered. "I think it used to belong to my grandfather. Yes, that's right. An old man gave it to him when he was young, but he couldn't read. My father showed it to me when I was a boy. I didn't know how to read then, either, and I guess he put it away. I had forgotten all about it. These look like plans of some kind."

"Plans for what?" asked a voice in the doorway.

Joseph Bonomi stood there, watching them stand over the trunk. In addition to being one of London's more celebrated architects, Bonomi was also going to back Sam financially on one of his inventions. Sam had scheduled a meeting with him to try and excite him about his latest discoveries.

"Mr. Bonomi!" said a startled Sam. "You're early!"

The pudgy Italian pulled out his pocket watch and wrinkled his brow.

"No, actually I'm five minutes late," he corrected him. "But that doesn't matter. Is that what you want to build with my money?"

"No—I mean yes," stammered Sam. No use ruling out anything that might help him shake a few pounds out of the old man.

"What is an 'NLE-13,' anyway?" asked Bonomi, looking through the spectacles that were pinching the end of his nose.

"Oh—um—" hesitated Sam.

Sensing her husband's uncertainty, Sarah stepped in.

"Mr. Bonomi, let me get you a cup of tea," she offered. "Would you care for a biscuit as well?"

"Oh, I shouldn't, Mrs. Warner," Bonomi smiled, patting his waist. "Trying to keep my weight down, you see. Uh—what kind of biscuits?"

She proceeded to bring out an assortment on a platter, and Bonomi took his time selecting four different cookies. Meanwhile, Sam took the opportunity to skim through the booklet and studied the pages of schematic diagrams at the end of it. By the time he was finished, he was visibly shaken. Fortunately, the others were too wrapped up in biscuit discussions to notice his stunned expression.

Sam did his best to regain his composure and cleared his throat.

"Oh, excuse me, Warner," mumbled Bonomi, his mouth filled with a bite of sugar cookie. "Just, uh, sampling a bit of your wife's baking. First rate, Mrs. Warner, first rate!"

Sarah excused herself and stepped back into the kitchen as Bonomi walked over and sat on the couch.

"Well, Warner, what new invention are you going to impress me with today?" he smiled, indicating for Sam to have a seat as well.

"Well sir, I know how the Duke of Wellington has been hoping for an explosive shell that might be used in naval battles," said Warner. "My design for such a torpedo is finished—"

"No, no, no," Bonomi cut him off. "Don't you know? They've started to build from DaVinci's plans. I heard yesterday that they're already testing them. What else have you got?"

Dammit, he thought. DaVinci had made life impossible for any enterprising inventor around London. The few things he hadn't built, he had designed, and the government was trying to develop them posthumously.

"Well, I'm in the early stages of developing a very small mine, one that can be placed underwater to secure shipping routes," he described.

"When will it be ready?" asked Bonomi.

"Uh... six months..." said Warner hopefully. "Maybe even sooner!"

"Let me know how you're doing in a few months," said the Italian, shifting in his seat restlessly. "Have you got anything else?"

Sam gulped. The baby would be along at any time, and he needed the money. With nothing to lose, he held up the NLE-13 Operator's Manual.

"Well, Mr. Bonomi," Sam hesitated, "I've saved the best for last. These are the plans for a real working time machine."

Bonomi looked at him, silent. Sam shifted in his seat. When it finally became apparent that Sam wasn't going to say more, Bonomi spoke.

"A time machine?" he said quietly, with just the barest hint of disbelief in his voice.

"That's right, sir," said Sam, eager for even that little bit of encouragement as he opened up the book to the pages in the rear. "Here are the plans for such a machine. Using this, one will be able to travel backwards and forwards in time!"

"A time machine," repeated Bonomi, more slowly this time.

"Can you imagine it?" enthused Sam. "Going back to view the wonders of the ancient world? Or seeing the world of tomorrow before your eyes?"

"And what makes you think it will work?" asked Bonomi.

"What makes—well, just look at those plans!" said Sam, recovering nicely. "Examine them for yourself! I will let them do my talking for me."

Bonomi poured over the diagrams, carefully studying each page. His skepticism appeared to lessen.

"Very interesting," he admitted.

"Just imagine being able to travel through time!" said Sam wistfully. "You could utilize the greatest scientific discoveries of any age! You could wipe out diseases! You could—"

"You could slit your enemies' throats in their cradles, before they grew up to bother you," said Bonomi. "You could pillage the greatest treasures of the past and become incredibly rich."

"Well—yes—in theory," said Sam, taken slightly aback at this unsavory turn.

"You know what a time machine like this would be worth?" asked Bonomi, his eyes growing wide. "Do you know how much money we could make if I sold something like this? Do you?"

"A lot?" answered Sam, panicking as conflicting emotions ran through his brain. His backer seemed to be quickly losing control.

"My boy, we'd be rich!" said Bonomi, his eyes now glazing over. "Can you imagine what you could do? What this would be worth to the right person?"

"B-but Mr. Bonomi," interjected Sam, "We have to build it first."

"Huh?" he asked, the spell momentarily broken. "Oh, oh yes. Build it. Right. Well, that shouldn't be a problem, should it?"

"We will need money," pointed out Sam. "Maybe a lot of money. Can you afford it?"

Bonomi looked at the plans, raising his left eyebrow.

"Hmm," he said, "I know somebody who can. Have you ever heard of Hannah Courtoy?"

Sam shook his head slowly.

"Not long after I got back from Egypt, I had a meeting with her. She was interested in funding another expedition, but I believe that His Majesty may have talked her out of it. You *do* know about Mrs. Courtoy and His Majesty?" said Bonomi in a low voice, dripping with innuendo.

There had indeed been talk around London, and Sam suddenly recognized the name of the reputed Royal Mistress of His Majesty, the late King William IV.

"Oh, yes, Mrs. Courtoy," he nodded solemnly.

"Filthy rich, dripping with money," he noted. "She has a couple of spinster daughters, I understand. I'll go give them a taste of the Bonomi charm, and we'll soon have all the money we need. Now you're sure you can build this? I've never heard of some of these materials."

"Oh, yes, it will be no problem at all," smiled Sam, the words "all the money we need" boosting his confidence considerably.

"Very good then, Sam, I shall talk with you soon," said Bonomi, rising and walking to the door. "Best of luck!"

The men shook hands and Bonomi disappeared into the bustling London streets. Sam closed the door and heaved a sigh, then sat back on the couch with the Manual in his lap.

Where would he ever get these parts? he wondered, paging through the manual. Of course he had never heard of these materials before—no one had, he was sure, except for the person who wrote this book. What was a "stabilizer?" An "energizer?" "Gyrogear?" "Power crystal?" He supposed he could start building what he could, and draw regular wages as long as possible. If Bonomi could indeed sweet-talk Hannah Courtoy into investing some of her sizeable fortune, he could probably make a decent living for quite some time. It was certainly worth a try anyway.

"Sarah!" he called to the kitchen. "I'll be in my workshop!"

Chapter Eleven

London 1848

London after dark was an astonishing sight.

Electricity had been commonplace for over 75 years, and the city was ablaze with brightly colored lights of all hues. Stan, Jack and Maggie walked along the sidewalks, with Maggie serving as their tour guide. After a short streetcar ride to the West End and the theatre district, they had decided to continue on foot.

"Before we had electric lights, most of the theatre productions were presented in the afternoon," she noted.

Stan and Jack barely noticed her as they gawked at the marquees, with the names of the theatres, plays and actors spelled out in flashing lights. The London Monorail that weaved above the streets was so radiant that it reminded the 21st Century travelers of a large neon tube.

"Excuse me!" she smiled. "You two look like you've never seen electric lights before! Don't they have electric lights in America?"

"Not like these..." marveled Jack.

They strolled near Piccadilly Circus, where the lights seemed even brighter. Not surprisingly, most were advertisements of some sort. Some things never change, Jack noted to himself as he studied the large Guinness sign that dominated several blocks.

Jack felt it was getting more and more difficult to lie to Maggie, and after talking it over with Stan, they had decided to tell her the truth. When she offered to show them around London, it seemed like the perfect opportunity. As electric trolley cars and monorails whizzed past them, Jack seized his chance.

"You know Maggie," he began, "We're actually not from America. Well, we are, but we aren't. Not from the America you know."

Maggie looked puzzled. When he saw how cute her freckled nose looked when she wrinkled it up that way, Jack almost chickened out.

"The America I know? What are you talking about?" she asked. "Do you mean you're from South America? Central America?"

"No, we're from North America, all right, we're just from the future—" blurted out Stan.

"The future of what?" she asked.

"Excuse my friend here," said Jack, shooting him a look that warned him to keep his mouth shut. Stan took the hint, feigning great interest in a hangnail as he dropped back slightly.

"What do you mean?" she puzzled. "You're ahead of your time or something?"

"Well, actually, it's the opposite," Jack hesitated. "We really do come from the future. We were born in the 21st Century."

"Y-you were, eh?" she asked, stopping short. Jack and Stan stopped in their tracks as well, and Jack suddenly wished they had kept their mouths shut.

"I know this sounds crazy, but it's true," said Jack. "We were born and raised in the 21st Century."

"You know this is the 19th Century?" she asked sharply. "And just how did you end up here?"

As Stan peered into a nearby shop window, Jack explained their story to her from the beginning, how the secret of time travel was discovered and how he ended up joining the Time Authority. Of course, he omitted a few details that did not reflect favorably on himself or his partner, but aside from that, he held nothing back. As he finished, Maggie backed away from him, her face a mixture of fear and concern.

"Let me make sure I understand something," she said slowly. "Has either of you two spent any time in an institution recently? Or maybe fallen and hurt your heads?"

"I know how crazy all this must sound—" blurted out Jack.

"Oh, do you?" she asked warily.

"Yes! Yes I do!" he answered. "So let me ask you something. If I do realize how crazy this all sounds—which I do—and I'm not mentally ill—which I'm not—then what reason could I possibly have for telling you such a wild story, unless it's the truth? What would I have to gain?"

Maggie stopped short. In an odd way, that did make sense. There truly was no reason for him to invent such a bizarre story, was there? Unless...

"Fine, I understand now," said Maggie. "I won't bother you any more."

A faint smile appeared on Jack's face. Then, Maggie walked to the curb and waved at an approaching trolley car.

"What are you doing?" he asked.

"I'm going home, and I would prefer that you two don't follow me," she said coolly.

"What are you talking about?" asked an astonished Jack. Stan looked up from his window-shopping in surprise.

"You can pick up your 'time machine' from the stable tomorrow," she said. "Don't bother asking for me, because I won't be home."

"Don't you believe me?" asked Jack.

The trolley car pulled up and Maggie stepped on board.

"Oh, of course I believe you," she said. "There isn't any reason to make up a wild story like that—unless you want to be rid of me, and you don't have the courage to simply say so. That's why I'm making it easy for you. Good-bye, Jack!"

And right on cue, as Maggie turned her back to them, the trolley car rolled off into the night.

"No, wait!" called Jack, starting after the trolley. "That's not true! Come back!"

But Jack, weaving his way through the crowds, was too slow, and the trolley proved too swift. Jack threw up his hands, then turned and walked back to Stan.

"Tough break," noted Stan.

"Why couldn't she believe me?" agonized Jack.

"You mean why couldn't she believe we were born 200 years in the future? And we zip around on Time Hoppers? How's that going to sound to someone from Victorian London?" asked Stan.

Jack heaved a sigh.

"You really like this girl?" said Stan.

Jack gave him a sheepish look.

"What are you doing? She's old enough to be your—well, you get the point!" lectured the agitated Stan. "You know the first rule of time travel! No interference! No—um—consorting with any of the life forms! You ought to be ashamed of yourself!"

"What for?"

"For what you were thinking!" said Stan. "You want to end up being your own great-great-great-great grandfather?"

"No!" sputtered Jack. "Of course not! I mean—well—"

Jack stopped in mid-sentence.

"Huh?" asked Stan.

"If we can't fix Nellie, we'll be stuck in this time period and none of this will matter anyway, right?" reasoned Jack.

"Right."

"But if we can fix her and this works out...we'll go back in time and correct the whole thing. We'll pick up DaVinci and take him back to the Sixteenth Century. And then none of this will have happened anyway," said Jack.

"What are you talking about?" asked Stan.

"I mean nothing that happens here and now will matter, because we're going to go back in time and nullify everything. Including Maggie..." Jack let his voice trail off.

"Maggie may not even exist..." said Stan, giving voice to their fears. "She might just be a part of this time bubble."

"Yes," said Jack, slowly and quietly. "And we're trying to pop it."

They both grew silent. This was something neither of them had considered. If they failed, they'd be stuck in the 19th Century. And if they succeeded, they could very well lose Maggie forever—they could literally wipe her out of existence.

"Is this what they mean by a time paradox?" asked Stan.

"I don't know," said Jack to himself, shaking his head and not listening to Stan.

"Here's something else we don't know," said Stan. "We don't have any more gold coins, it's late at night and we don't know where we are. So where are we going to sleep tonight?"

And as the two men looked at each other, a cold drizzle began to fall.

Chapter Twelve

London 1768

In no time at all, the Court of King George III had begun to turn on Benjamin Franklin. It had all started with the "stolen plans" allegation, and escalated from there. His Majesty had grown increasingly paranoid of everyone around him—except for Lord North and DaVinci—and the moment the court gossips first spread the word of Franklin's "accusations," the King had leveled his beady eyes on the American. From that moment on, everything Franklin said, wrote, or invented was viewed with suspicion by His Majesty and everyone else who wanted to curry favor with the Monarch.

Franklin himself became increasingly uncomfortable in Court. Invitations to the best parties had dried up, folks had stopped laughing at his jokes, and worst of all, certain ladies had begun refusing their services—and his money. It was rumored that he was no longer welcome at the notorious Hellfire Club. In short, Franklin saw himself becoming a pariah.

After their encounter regarding the electrical plans, DaVinci kept himself quite detached from the American. No one in court would have ever suspected that those machinations threatening Franklin were being fueled by DaVinci. The Italian was careful to stay far from the fray when things got ugly. In fact, he often went out of his way to deliver backhanded compliments, or damn him with faint praise.

DaVinci was determined to craft himself a reputation as a wit, as well as an artistic and scientific genius, and was not reticent to do so at the expense of the American. After an informal reading by Franklin of some of his writings—which was met with the politest of applause—DaVinci whispered one of his most-quoted lines to the Duchess of Westminster. "It sounds like Dr. Franklin is as good at his writing as he is at his burglary," he told her with eyes twinkling. DaVinci knew that the second-most effective way of kicking off a smear campaign in London was to print up thousands of handbills and scatter them all over town. The most effective way was telling the Duchess. And in less than 24 hours, DaVinci's bon mot was whispered in the finest salons and drawing rooms in London.

DaVinci sat in His Majesty's drawing room, where each of them was quaffing a large mug of ale. The King had called him for an audience, which, despite his familiarity with the monarch, was not an everyday occurrence. They made small talk about a few minor ongoing scandals, while DaVinci wondered about the real purpose of his visit.

After finishing his second ale, the King focused on his guest.

"So, it sounds like our Dr. Franklin is causing quite a commotion," he began.

"How is that, Your Majesty?" asked DaVinci. He had learned that it was always better to discern the King's opinion as quickly as possible in order to more fully agree with him. With the Royal Dementia on the rise lately, it never hurt to be as solicitous as possible.

"People are talking about him," he said. "Remember, he is an American. Can't trust him."

"No, Your Majesty," said DaVinci. "Still, he is very clever."

"Just so, DaVinci, just so!" exclaimed the King. "Too clever by half!"

"Yes, Your Majesty," said DaVinci, not sure what that was supposed to mean or where the conversation was heading. "Very well respected."

"And that's the problem!" he grumbled. "He's a troublemaker, but too many people like him."

"Your Majesty?" asked DaVinci.

"Can't do a bloody thing to him," said the King. "He throws the Court into an uproar, but he has too many friends. Can't throw him into the Tower. Can't cut off his head. Er—can I?"

"Well—no, that probably wouldn't be a good idea, Your Majesty," said DaVinci.

"But we need to deal with him," he noted. "What do you think, Signor DaVinci? Can you help me with this?"

"Uh—well, yes, Your Majesty," he said. "I'll do anything I can."

The Monarch knitted his ale-addled brow in thought.

"Hmmm..." he mused. "He is American. Supposing he was spying for them? Perhaps he is going to betray us?"

"Yes, Your Majesty," said a relieved DaVinci. "That is food for thought. Let me see what I can do..."

Franklin knew something was wrong, but he wasn't completely sure why it was happening. Was it his imagination, or were people gossiping behind his back? At any rate, he needed some sound advice—or at least a sounding board—but no one seemed to be available to meet with him. His access to the King and Lord North had been abruptly severed, and none of the aristocracy or M.P.s seemed to have any use for him, either. His one chance, his only remaining contact with the King's Inner Circle, the only person still willing to meet with him, was his fellow scientist, Signor DaVinci.

In fact, DaVinci seemed almost eager to help. They had been friendly rivals in recent months for the King's attentions, and Franklin sometimes thought the Italian was jealous of him, but his suggestion that they meet for tea was warmly received. Perhaps he had misjudged him, thought Franklin, and as he nervously adjusted the table settings for the tenth time that afternoon, his manservant Eric stepped in.

"Signor Leonardo DaVinci to see you, sir," he announced.

"Ah yes, very good," said Franklin. "Send him in, Eric!"

The servant stepped into the hallway, and a moment later DaVinci entered the room, a beatific smile on his face.

Beaming, Franklin walked over to him with his hand outstretched.

"Signor DaVinci, it is wonderful to see you!" said Franklin grabbing his hand and pumping it anxiously. "Thank you for accepting my invitation!"

"And thank you for extending your kind invitation," said the Italian.

Franklin, still shaking his hand, led him over to the table and held out a chair for him while DaVinci sat. Franklin moved around to the other side of the table and took the seat opposite the Old Man.

"This is the finest wine in Britain," he noted, smiling as he poured DaVinci a glass. As he poured, he suddenly realized that his invitation was to tea and gave a nervous start, but continued pouring and trusted that the Italian wouldn't mind. "I think you will find this better than any tea I might serve you."

"Yes, I'm sure, Dr. Franklin, but I am an ordinary man with ordinary tastes," said DaVinci, grabbing the glass before Franklin could replace it with tea. "I do not need expensive wines."

"Oh, no, of course not," said the American, making a mental note to bring out the cheap stuff if he should ever entertain the ungrateful bastard again. "I asked you here because, frankly, I need to ask you something in strictest confidence."

The Italian took a sip from his glass. Not bad, he thought.

"Of course," said DaVinci, "You may tell me anything and be assured that I will hold it in strictest confidence."

"I appreciate that, Signor DaVinci," said Franklin. "I must confess, I need your help."

"I am at your service," he responded, trying to hide his insincerity.

"Perhaps it is my imagination, but I have noticed that—certain elements in the King's Court seem to hold me in disfavor," said Franklin.

The Old Man raised his eyebrows slightly, indicating for him to continue.

"I mean to say—there seem to be people whispering behind my back, passing on untruths, gossip, innuendoes," he said. "I have not been invited to a party in over a month, and my presence is no longer requested at any meetings of the palace advisors. I know that many people consider you and I to be rivals for the King's attentions, but we know that not to be true. In fact, I consider you to be one of my closest friends in London."

What a wretched man if that is the case, thought DaVinci.

"And that is why I ask you, as a friend, to speak up, to offer me counsel," said Franklin. "I must know why I am being held in such disapproval, and what I can do to prevent it. Frankly, I would rather die than remain in the King's disfavor this way."

Slowly, the Italian took another sip of wine, let it rest on his palate for a moment, and then swallowed.

"You are correct," said DaVinci.

Franklin gasped.

"I—see," he stammered.

"I repeat, 'You are correct,' Dr. Franklin," said DaVinci. "It most certainly is your imagination."

"It is?" he asked.

"Of course. You are one of His Majesty's most loyal subjects, and I see no reason for your feelings of inadequacy," said DaVinci.

"But—but the parties—"

"What parties? There have been no parties in the past month—at least, none worthy of our attendance," said DaVinci.

Desperate to believe him, Franklin began to rationalize all that he had seen and heard during the past few weeks. Perhaps

His Majesty and the others had simply been pre-occupied as of late. It was true that no one had been discourteous to his face. Still—

"Didn't the Duke and Duchess of Oxford have some sort of party not long ago?" he asked hesitantly.

"That dreadful thing?" DaVinci rolled his eyes. "I had to go—I could not come up with an excuse. You know what a crashing bore all of their parties are."

"Oh, uh, yes, yes," said Franklin, who had actually had a delightful time at their last party, but wanted to trust him.

"As a matter of fact," he lied as he leaned over to Franklin and lowered his voice, "I saw your name on their guest list and took the liberty of mentioning that you had been unwell as of late. I felt I was doing you a favor, but I fear I over-stepped—"

"No, no! Not at all!" said Franklin. He had heard rumors that DaVinci was badmouthing him to the Duke and Duchess, but was relieved to discover the truth. Though he would have loved to have attended the party, if they were being viewed as less than desirable hosts—

"I owe you a debt of gratitude," said a smiling Franklin, but was struck by another thought. "But when I last visited Mrs. Gabler's establishment—I was told I was not welcome..."

Mrs. Gabler, who operated one of the most exclusive cathouses in all of London, had indeed excluded the American from her house of ill repute after talking to DaVinci; she feared Franklin's recent notoriety might tarnish her reputation and hurt business.

"Yes—well—may I be frank?" he asked.

"Of course, of course!" urged Franklin.

"Well, it seems that some of the ladies—they are offended..."

"Offended?" asked the puzzled American.

"Your smell..." whispered DaVinci. "They found it offensive. Perhaps more frequent bathing—a different soap?"

Franklin sniffed himself several times, as the Italian tried not to laugh.

"Oh! I am mortified!" he said.

"I am sorry, but I felt we were close enough to be perfectly honest."

"Oh yes, yes! I thank you very much!" said the flustered American.

DaVinci gave a benign smile, trying not to burst out laughing. He had just told Franklin he smelled, and the idiot was thanking him. In fact, the American used too many perfumes and scented soaps, and if anything, increasing his dosage would make him even less popular.

"My pleasure, and I hope I have been of some help," said DaVinci. He drained his glass and then stood.

"Oh, yes, very much so! Thank you again, Signor!"

DaVinci raised his hand to shake, but the American embraced him instead. The Italian gave him a perfunctory pat on the back, and stepped back.

"I am so lucky to have a friend like you," said Franklin sincerely.

"You are too kind, Dr. Franklin," he smiled as he walked to the door and opened it to exit. "Too kind."

Chapter Thirteen

1848

Stan and Jack woke up in an alley a few blocks off Piccadilly. A light drizzle was still falling. Though they had attempted to huddle inside an alcove, they were too large to fit, and a steady dripping had soaked them completely. They each stretched their limbs, moaned and stood unsteadily, feeling thoroughly defeated.

"Well, now what?" asked Jack. "We're lost, broke, wet, hungry, and Maggie thinks we're a pair of lunatics."

"Maybe we'll feel better if we eat a little breakfast," suggested Stan.

A few wooden boards suddenly slid off another alcove nearby, and a few similarly disheveled men in ragged clothing climbed out. They scattered out into the already bustling street, except for a man with short grey hair and an unkempt salt-and-pepper colored beard. He shot them an angry glance and called to them in a loud whisper.

"You two better keep it down, or Specserv's gonna round all of us up!" he warned in a low, angry growl. "You new? I ain't seen you around."

"Uh—sort of," said Stan.

"Americans, eh? Well, if you want to become old, don't let Specserv find you sleeping on the streets," he said. "You'll disappear, and nobody'll ever see you again!"

Before his warning had completely sunk in, he was gone.

"He's probably just trying to scare us," said Stan.

"Well," said Jack, "It's working."

"I think we'll have to go back and find Maggie somehow," said Stan.

Deep in his heart, that was what Jack wanted more than anything, but some strange feeling in his gut—pride, perhaps?—would not allow him.

"No, no," he said. "She already thinks we're completely mad."

"But what else can we do?" asked Stan, holding his palms up in a gesture of futility. "We can't stay here. We don't have any money. We don't have any food."

"All right, all right," admitted Jack. "I suppose we could try to find our way back there and get Nellie. There has to be some way to put her back together."

"We need to find the Manual," said Stan. "If we can get her running again, we can fix everything."

"And if we can't," said Jack, "everything we know will be wiped out."

Maggie sat on a bench in the back of the stable, picking through the pile of rubble deposited by Stan and Jack. The large framework was twisted, the metal bent or snapped at the joints, just the sort of quality one might expect for a project awarded to the lowest bidder. It would be considered shoddy construction for a flying machine expected to take its share of stress and rough landings, though perfectly reasonable for a machine that is transported—or teleported—through space and time. She laughed at the thought, then reached down and tried to straighten a piece of the silvery metal which she failed to recognize as aluminum. It snapped off in her hand. The damage to the fragile craft appeared to be far too extensive to repair, and she weighed the idea of throwing everything in the trash heap out back.

She lifted another length of the shiny metal, and found a large surface with a flat greenish square in the middle, surrounded by dials, levers, and all manner of switches, the likes of which she had never before seen.

Why had they been so careful to recover each fragment? she wondered as she studied the wreckage. *And what is this metal, shiny and lightweight, yet strong until bent?*

Maggie noticed a crystal the size of her fist. In the dim light in the back of the stable, it was glowing with a faint greenish light, and she tapped it quickly and cautiously. There seemed to be no ill effects, and so she picked it up. It was smooth to the touch, and surprisingly cool. She held it up and peered at it as daylight streamed in through a crack in the ceiling, and it seemed to glow even brighter.

If this was a fake, then how? And why? Why go through all of this trouble to construct a phony "time machine," only to hide it away where no one but she could see it? Thanks to James, she had become familiar enough with state-of-the-art flying machines to recognize that this was not one of them. Maggie was not the sharpest knife in the kitchen, but she was far from the dullest, and it began to strike her that the wreckage before her might—just might—be what Stan and Jack claimed it to be. It was all rather unsettling.

Maggie placed the glowing crystal down with the smaller wreckage, and after a moment's thought, covered it with a handful of straw to conceal the greenish glow. As she brushed her hands against her dress to knock the straw loose, Wally entered the stable and walked back to join her.

"Did your friends leave?" he asked.

Deep in thought, she had not heard him approach and gave a sudden start.

"Wally!" she said. "I—didn't know you were there!"

"Just got in, Miss Maggie," he said, smiling. "Them American fellas left and stuck you with their junk, huh?"

"Something like that," she answered.

"Want me to throw it out?" he asked.

Maggie paused for a moment then shook her head.

"I think we'll hold onto it just a little longer," she said. "Maybe tomorrow. Yes. I'll throw it out tomorrow."

The valet helped Joseph Bonomi with his hat and cloak, slipping the latter over his shoulders and fastening it at the neck.

"Thank you, Jones," he said as the servant handed him his cane.

Bonomi cut a rather dashing figure in his waistcoat. Like its wearer, it was well worn, yet held up well for its age.

Fortunately, both the gentleman and the formalwear cleaned up very well when necessary, because it had been an important meeting. Though Mrs. Courtoy—Hannah—may have been anticipating a date, Bonomi had been relentless in his mission. He had to charm, cajole, flatter and seduce the dried-up old thing into investing a considerable sum of money in an unbelievable enterprise. If it succeeded, they would all be wealthy beyond their wildest dreams, though the chances of that were admittedly slim. Bonomi rationalized that she wouldn't even miss the money when—if it failed, and she would be getting a few final thrills on her way to the cemetery.

"If you think this is a sound enterprise, Mr. Bonomi, then I shall trust to your good judgment," she told him, leaving him feeling simultaneously exhilarated and guilt-ridden.

He mumbled something about the potential rewards far exceeding the risks, and she bought it. The old woman had always regretted not investing in his Egyptian expedition to the Valley of Kings. Its success had brought his backers tremendous acclaim and plenty of potential reflected glory in which she was unable to bask, and so made her particularly susceptible to any investment Bonomi might offer.

If only she didn't have those two daughters, he thought to himself. They were unattractive, unpleasant and unmarried; they could not change the first trait, had no interest in softening the second, but the entire household seemed to be obsessed with altering the third. At one point, he was forced to make an impassioned declaration on the separation of business and personal relationships, which he thought would scotch the whole deal, but after brief consideration, she agreed to invest.

Bonomi felt he was a little too young for the mother, and a little too old for the daughters, but the Courtoy family seemed to be interested in any warm body in pants, and even that point did not seem to be set in stone.

But the mission was successful, and Hannah Courtoy had written him a cheque right then and there, so the construction could begin. Warner would be elated. And if it was a success, the sky would truly be the limit. Admiral Joseph Bonomi—well, that might do for a start.

Still, as he walked briskly along the street, he couldn't help but feel badly for Mrs. Courtoy. If she couldn't marry herself or her daughters off with the dowries she could offer, there was even less hope than currently existed. There were still some things he would not do for money, and the Courtoy sisters were two of them.

Sam Warner called Sarah out to the old coach house behind their home that he now considered his workshop. Although they'd had a carriage and horse several years ago, time—and eight children—had taken their toll. The horse had died, and the carriage had fallen into such disrepair that he could not sell it for what he knew it was worth. Ultimately, that proved a lucky break.

Sarah stepped into the coach house-turned-workshop and gasped.

"What have you been doing in here?" she gasped.

After only a few short days, the only recognizable sights in the workshop were Sam and the remnants of their old carriage. Everywhere else were scraps of metal, tools and bits of wire. Schematic diagrams were tacked up that virtually covered the walls. Sitting on the floor, where the horse would normally be hitched, was a large device that looked and sounded like a hydraulic engine.

In the center of the room sat the bits and pieces of their carriage. The frame had apparently been reinforced with narrow iron beams, and the driver's seat had been removed. In its place was a bank of switches and primitive levers, and below that a battery for generating electricity, apparently for the lights that pointed out in all directions.

And there were wires everywhere. There were wires leading from the engine to the control panel to the battery, wires connecting the battery to the lights, wires connecting the lights to the control panel, and wires from the control panel to the round metallic globe on top.

Sam was lying on his back underneath the control panel, reaching up under the console, with a set of plans propped up next to his head. Upon hearing his wife's voice, he pushed himself out from beneath the wiring, craning his neck up and forcing a smile on his face.

"Oh, hello Sarah. I...didn't know you were here."

"What is all this? What have you done to the carriage?"

"You mean this old thing?" he smiled. "Well, we haven't used it since the horse died, and we talked about getting a motorcar—"

"Will you tell me how we're going to afford a motorcar when you waste all of your time on these impossible gadgets?"

"Well, we could sell the carriage—"

"Like this?" she exploded. "You couldn't sell it before—what makes you think tearing it apart and wrapping it up with metal and wires is going to increase its re-sale value?"

"But Sarah, you don't understand," said Sam, trying to calm her. "Bonomi and his investors are paying me to do this—"

"And what happens when this time machine of yours is a big flop?"

"Sarah, why are you always so negative?"

"Sam, you found all of this, all of these plans, in a book that your grandfather claims he found as a child," she explained slowly. "If it could really work—if it had any value at all—don't you think somebody would have invented it in the past 75 years? This is just a work of fiction, of someone's overactive imagination, and you are taking it far too seriously."

"Darling, you haven't studied these drawings too closely," he said, picking them up and holding them in front of her. "At first, I was just going to do this and collect on my wages. I was just as skeptical as you were, but then I started studying. And you know what? It could work. The scientific principles are sound. There are only a few obstacles I need to overcome—"

"If it does work, you'll probably find out DaVinci already built one," she said, a reference to a torpedo that Sam had designed for the Royal Navy, only to find they were already testing a similar design invented by the Italian.

Sarah snatched the plans from his hand and studied them for a moment. Sam pointed out a few features.

"See, I'm using the hydraulic engine instead of this power source, and I can draw enough electricity from the battery to operate the instrument display board for a few moments," he enthused.

"That's all well and good, Sam, but how are you going to travel through time? Where is your 'stabilizer?'" she asked, reading terms from the plans. "How about a 'gyrogear' or an 'energizer?'"

"I'm not worrying about that right now," he said. "I'm putting together as much as I can, and then I'll have to find substitutes for a few of the more unusual materials."

"Do you even know what a 'power crystal' is?" she asked plaintively.

"Of course!" he snapped, then hesitated. "It's, uh, a crystal-looking thing about as big as my fist. And, when it's full of power, it's supposed to have a sort of green-ish glow to it."

Sarah studied him. He was still the man she loved, but he was maddening at times. At that moment, she didn't know whether to pound on his chest in frustration or throw her arms around him. She finally shook her head, recognizing it as a lost cause.

"Fine," she said. "I'll pick you up one next time I go to market. And a couple of stabilizers."

Chapter Fourteen

1848

The Specserv forces were closing in on Stan and Jack. The pair had managed to elude the agents for the past two days, but they could not show their faces in the daytime or at night without attracting suspicious glances. Jack had devised a plan to steal a pair of British Empire uniforms from a local laundress, but was thwarted by the unexpected arrival of the clothing's owner, a six-foot four-inch 240-pound Specserv Major. Stan and Jack were able to flee, but not before the Major got a good look at them. Soon the lampposts of London were plastered with remarkably good likenesses of the pair, promising rewards for information leading to their capture.

Which was why they were forced into hiding, living in the shadows as they searched desperately for Maggie's home. They were soon aware of how large London had become, and how much the rows of houses all resembled each other. They confined their movements to the back alleys while they looked for any familiar landmarks. Occasionally, they would take a chance and ask for directions to the Wells house, but were met by blank stares most of the time.

Finally, on the morning of the third day, Jack discreetly approached a businessman after first checking the area for Specserv agents and wanted posters.

"Scuse me, squire, I'm lookin' for the Wells house," he asked in a low voice and the best British accent he could muster.

"Two blocks down, middle of the second block, number 82," the man replied without looking up.

When he and Stan arrived, it turned out to be an engineering office.

"We came this far," shrugged Stan, and they entered.

A rather meek man was sitting at a desk by the front door.

"What can I do to help you gentlemen?" he asked.

"We were looking for the Wells house," said Stan.

"Yes, this is the place," said the man. "And where would you like your well dug?"

"No, we don't want a well dug—well—I mean—" stammered an immediately confused Stan.

"But—all of our wells are dug very well indeed—I mean to say—they are fine quality—" stammered the man at the desk.

"What's the matter, Frank?" asked a rather burly man sitting further inside.

"Something wrong with our wells?" threatened an even larger man, with an ominous edge to his voice.

Jack bristled, sensing a music hall routine with the potential for immediate violence. He would have to intervene, or at least make an attempt. The last thing they needed was a public scene.

"What my friend was just saying is that you dig the finest wells in all of Britain," said Jack shamelessly.

"So what sort of well do you want us to dig?" asked the burly man.

"I don't need one of your wells—" said Jack, immediately regretting his choice of words.

"Oh you don't, eh?" asked the larger man, rising and taking a step in their direction. "And what's wrong with our wells?"

"N-nothing!" stammered Stan.

"And yet you don't want one!" said the burly man, taking a couple of steps in their direction.

"No! I mean—yes! But not now!" Stan protested.

The two men, now joined by a third, began advancing toward Stan and Jack.

"You salespeople are really persistent," Jack mumbled to himself, as he and Stan started backing toward the door.

"Stop right there!" called the third man, and Stan and Jack bolted toward the door.

The chase was on. The three muscular engineers dashed toward them, but lost valuable moments when Stan slammed the door in their faces. They threw it open and the largest cried "Stop them! Someone stop them!"

"Stop them?" For what? Not buying something is a crime in this world? Jack thought to himself as they ran.

Stan had a slight lead, and Jack struggled to keep up, even though his lungs were burning. Neither looked back to check on their pursuers, but they could hear the commotion in their wake. Stan took a sudden right and turned down another street, with Jack right on his heels.

"We've—got to—lose these guys!" Jack huffed and puffed, knowing he couldn't keep up his pace much longer.

"Any ideas?" gasped Stan.

Panicking, Jack quickly surveyed the street ahead. Nothing. A few children watched them run past, as did a figure standing in the shadows between buildings. As they approached the entrance to an alley on the right, Jack called to his partner.

"Up here! Take a right!" he choked.

With no hesitation, Stan immediately dashed into the alley, followed by Jack, just as their pursuers turned the previous corner. Had they been spotted?

About 50 feet ahead was a motorized wagon ahead filled with coal.

"In there!" Jack indicated. "Hide!"

Stan gave a quick, distasteful moan. He didn't like the idea, but didn't have a better choice with the authorities breathing down their necks. Still at a full run, he took a few more steps, then sprang up and into the load of coal. He winced as he hit the rocks, though his forward momentum made it easier to bear.

Just as he started to turn, Jack came leaped in beside him, suppressing a pained grunt as he landed.

"Let's get out of sight," Jack whispered. He began rolling from side to side, burrowing himself deeper and deeper into the load of coal, as he scooped out handfuls of rock from beneath him.

Stan sullenly followed his lead and began burying himself in the back of the wagon, likewise scooping handfuls of coal from under him and piling them on the exposed areas of his body. In just a few moments, they had largely succeeded, but their hearts were in their throats. The heavy boot heels of their pursuers rounded the corner and headed down the alley in their direction. Stan and Jack were each careful to quietly burrow down even further into the pile, hoping against hope that the authorities would give up their chase. To their extreme chagrin, the pursuers came to a halt a few feet away from the pair.

"Must've got away, Burton," said one voice.

"Hmmm... I'm not so sure, Cheswick," surmised the other one. "Let's take a look in here."

Jack's heart was in his throat. They would have no trouble finding him as he cowered a few feet away from them, separated only by a few nuggets of coal.

"Have your firearms ready," cautioned the second voice.

Though he couldn't allow himself to peek out, Jack could almost feel the gun pointing directly at him.

"Don't worry, sir," said the first voice. "I see anything funny, I shoot first, and ask questions later."

The second man grabbed one side of the bed of the motorcar and pulled himself in with the coal. A worn shovel was propped up against the side, which the second man grabbed. He picked it up and threw it over his shoulder, but before he could bring it down sharply on their bodies, another voice called out.

"James! There's another group of them that rode off that way!" she shouted.

After only a moment's hesitation, the second man clambered out of the motorcar and jumped to the ground.

"What's that? Maggie?" he asked.

"The two men!" she replied. "The two men you were chasing. They went that way! Be careful, James, they look dangerous!"

Upon hearing her familiar voice, Jack began to smile in spite of their situation.

"Yes. Yes, of course. Maggie, I—I'll talk to you later," said the voice, apparently that of her quasi-boyfriend. He hesitated, and then the two of them started running off in the direction that Maggie had pointed.

Stan and Jack kept still under the shallow covering of coal as they heard their two pursuers' footsteps fade into the distance. Then they heard the closest pair of footsteps begin walking away from them. Jack pushed himself into a sitting position, letting the coal roll off him and into the back of the wagon, where it partially filled the hollow he had wriggled out for himself. Stan sat up a moment later.

"That was Maggie!" he gasped.

"I know," said Jack.

Stan began knocking the coal dust off his shirtsleeves; it came off in black clouds. Much of it settled on his shirt and pants, and his face and hands were nearly covered with the greasy black powder as well.

Jack was neither better nor any cleaner, but he had no time for grooming. He peered over the edge of the wagon and saw the familiar form of Maggie Wells walking away from them.

"Psst! Maggie!" he called in his best approximation of a stage whisper, hoping to get her attention even though James Burton might still be within earshot.

She continued walking. If she had heard him, she didn't intend to let him know. A couple of feet away from Jack, Stan peered over the side as well.

"Maggie!" he said in a slightly louder tone. "Is that you? What are you doing?"

Maggie stopped short, then turned around. Upon seeing their blackened faces, she stifled an urge to laugh out loud, and maintained her strict composure.

"Well, apparently I'm finding the time and water to bathe somewhat more regularly than other people," she said with a strict look on her face.

"Yeah, but we had to hide fast," admitted Stan.

"So I guessed," she said. "I see that your—partner—is still with you."

Jack smiled a dirty, sickly-looking smile in her direction.

"Uh—thank you Maggie," he said politely. "Thanks for helping us get away."

"That's all right, Jack," she said, allowing a break in her reserve. "I suppose I did overreact."

"Well, that's understandable," said Jack. "After all, we were asking you to believe something that must sound impossible. Or insane."

"True," she said, a tiny smile creeping across her face.

"You don't still think we're insane, do you?" asked Stan.

"Don't push your luck."

"Look, I guess the only way we can convince you is to show you," said Jack. "To re-build Nellie—the Time Machine—and demonstrate it."

"You don't have to convince me or demonstrate anything," said Maggie. "It doesn't matter. I'm trying hard to believe you, I really am. The truth of it is, I don't know what to believe. But it doesn't matter. I still like you, and, for some reason, I still trust you. And, I'll help you if I can."

Stan and Jack clambered out of the back of the wagon and started walking toward her.

"Thanks, Maggie," said Stan. "You're the best."

"I don't even know what to say," said Jack, looking into her eyes. "I've never met another woman like you."

"There isn't another woman like me," she corrected.

Jack reached out and grabbed her hand gently, then held it up and cupped it with his other hand. They smiled and gazed at each other, until Jack suddenly broke the moment by looking down at his coal dust-covered hands embracing her delicate white skin. They each gave a start, and he immediately threw down her hand and backed up a step.

"Look, we'd better get you two hidden away somewhere," she said. "Those two could come back at any time. Now follow me."

Stan snapped into lockstep beside her as she began walking swiftly toward the street. Jack stood there for a moment, stunned, as a thought struck him. Then he hurried to catch up with the other two as they walked swiftly along.

"Who was that?" he asked.

"Who was who?"

"That guy! He's the one, isn't he?"

Maggie raised an eyebrow.

"You know what I mean!" said Jack. "Your boyfriend, that James Burton! That's the reason he and the other soldier left so fast, isn't it?"

"Mr. Burton used to call on me, yes," she answered a bit guardedly. "But I have no idea why he left so quickly. Maybe he just believed me."

"Oh, right," said Jack suspiciously.

"And he isn't my 'boyfriend,'" she said, a hint of anger slipping into her voice. "And that's my choice, not his, not since he joined Specserv. But unless you want to keep sleeping in alleyways, I shouldn't bring it up again if I were you."

Jack bit his tongue as they continued walking, Stan and Jack on either side of Maggie.

"Drop back," she whispered to them both.

"What?" asked Stan, slowing enough to let her take the lead by a half dozen feet.

"I don't exactly look like I belong next to the two of you, now, do I?" she answered.

"What's that supposed to mean?" asked Jack, feeling even more hurt and confused.

"It means I don't want to look suspicious or call attention to the three of us," she answered. "You look like a couple of chimney sweeps. There's no reason for a lady to be seen walking with a chimney sweep."

"Not even if I was sweeping your chimney?" asked Stan.

Maggie turned to her side and stared at him, and Stan dropped back a few steps.

"Don't be acting all put out, please," she said, a bit more gently. "This is nothing personal. I'm just trying to keep you two alive!"

Jack smiled. She was right and they were overreacting.

"Sorry..." he mumbled, and the two chimney sweeps from the future followed Maggie back to her stable.

The junkman pushed his cart along the back street.

"Any rags? Any scrap metal?" he called out as he slowly ambled along.

Wally looked out from the stable as Burt the junkman came closer. Then, he looked back at the pile of scrap. Maggie did tell him they'd be throwing it out today...

"Mornin' Burt!"

"Mornin' Wally," he answered. "Anything today?"

Wally looked down, deep in thought.

"Well, I'm not sure," he said. "Miss Maggie was going to have something, but—can you come back tomorrow?"

"I can try," said Burt. "What have you got?"

"Broken down flying machine," said Wally, as he stepped over to the wreckage and picked up a piece to show Burt.

"That won't be goin' anywhere," chuckled Burt.

As Wally set the piece of metal down on the straw, he felt it hit something, and bent over to pick up the power crystal.

"Wouldja look at that!" gasped Burt.

The greenish glow of the crystal was easy to spot in the shadows of the stable, despite the sunlight that was now peeking through the many cracks.

"Yeah, Maggie was lookin' at this thing, too," said Wally. "I reckon you can pick this up when you pick up the rest of this junk, but I bet you'll have to pay a bit extra for this beauty."

Burt said nothing, mesmerized by the glowing crystal as Wally placed it on the ground.

"I have to run into the house," said Wally, "But can you be sure to come back tomorrow? I really gotta check with Miss Maggie."

"Yeah, yeah, sure," said the distracted Burt. "I'll be back in the morning..."

Burt started pushing his cart away, while Wally headed toward the Wells house. As soon as Wally was out of sight, Burt stopped. He listened carefully for a moment, then tiptoed over to the stable. He slipped inside and picked up the power crystal from the ground. His fascination with the crystal far outweighed any ethical questions, and he stuffed it into his shirt. Looking around but spotting no one, Burt headed back to his cart.

"What difference does it make whether I take it today or tomorrow?" he thought to himself. "I ought to be able to collect plenty for this, and I can pay Wally his share tomorrow. He can't be upset about that, and nobody'll be any the wiser."

Chapter Fifteen

1848

A few minutes later, Maggie stepped into the stable, followed closely by Stan and Jack. She glanced around, relieved to see that Wally wasn't there. She didn't feel up to the explanations yet.

"Make yourselves comfortable," she gestured with a sweeping motion of her hand. "It may be a bit messy, but it should be safe. If anybody asks—"

"Tell them we're escaped fugitives, and you're helping us?" joked Jack.

"Yes, that's right," she smiled. "Seriously, James—my ex-boyfriend—may decide this is a good week to visit me, and it won't look good if I'm harboring the fugitives he was trying to capture."

The two men looked for a relatively clean place, spotting the wreckage of Nellie.

"Why don't we try to do some work on Nellie here while we're waiting?" asked Stan.

"I guess it can't hurt," said Jack. "I don't think we'll be able to do much without the manual, though."

"But try to keep the noise down," said Maggie. "I'll have Wally bring you some soap and water so you can wash some of that soot off."

Maggie walked back to her house and disappeared inside. Stan and Jack watched her go, and then turned their attention to the business at hand. With the doors to the stable closed to conceal them from the occasional passer-by (or Specserv agent), the pair began pulling out pieces of the wreckage one by one.

The large pieces of the frame appeared to be twisted or broken in pieces. Time Hoppers were never designed to take much physical, non-time-traveling abuse, and falling less than ten feet did a surprising amount of structural damage.

The control panel itself seemed to be in fairly good shape, though the wiring beneath appeared to be disconnected or even sheared off in spots, and Jack remembered yanking out a handful of wires to get it to stop. Luckily the circuit boards looked to be intact; those would be difficult to replace. The stabilizer looked none the worse for wear. Stan picked up the homing beacon that had, unbeknownst to them, caused so many problems. The tiny wire loop antenna that stuck out of the top had come loose, also unknown to them, because Leonardo DaVinci had been trying to use it for a handhold. Stan fed half the length of the wire back into the casing and studied his repair job with a satisfied look. If it had been hooked up to a power source, Mr. Hodges and Corporal Spumoni would have been able to track them from headquarters.

But the drive mechanism was the biggest challenge. The fall had scattered those components in all directions. Fortunately, none of them appeared to be seriously damaged. The casing of the gyrogear had a small crack running through it, but it was nothing that couldn't be fixed with a bit of duct tape. The energizer looked to be in even better shape, though it was obviously out of power. Still, there had to be enough electrical power available to charge it up in this version of the 19th Century, hadn't there?

The bad news, Jack thought to himself, is that they would desperately need the manual to successfully re-wire the console and reassemble the drive mechanism.

"There's a rip in the upholstery," pointed out Stan. "That's your seat."

"Let's lay these out on the ground so we can see what we have," said Jack.

The two of them began laying out the pieces on the dirt floor as if they were preparing to assemble the machine. When they finished, the parts covered an area ten feet square. They stepped back and began surveying the situation.

"Do you remember how the undercarriage is supposed to look?" asked Stan.

"I think the power cables ran along here lengthwise, going from the power crystal to—" Jack said, stopping short as he noticed something missing. Something important.

"The power crystal—" said Jack.

"Huh?"

"It's gone!"

"It can't be," said Stan. "I remember bringing it in here. There was still some juice left in it."

By this time, Jack had begun frantically searching the stable, looking high, low, in corners, and under the clutter and discarded carriage parts that had gathered over the years.

"If we've lost that, we're stuck!" Jack said nervously. "In every sense of the word..."

Stan joined in the search, starting with the larger stall that housed the Wells' family's horseless carriage. Soon, they were both on their hands and knees in the muddy second stall, sifting through the straw by the fistful.

"It's got to be here!" Jack protested. "It can't just disappear."

"It's gone," said Stan. "I'm starting to recognize these clumps of mud by now."

Stan reached out and grabbed a boot. He looked up and saw it was attached to a leg. He continued his upward gaze and saw Wally staring back at him. Wally was carrying two buckets of water, one in each hand.

"If you didn't roll around in the manure that way, you probably wouldn't need so much washing up," he told them derisively.

Stan and Jack looked at each other, deciding there was no point in more searching. Wally handed them lumps of soap, and with the stable doors closed, they stripped down and started washing off the coal dust, straw, and dried-up mud. Jack stuck his head in his basin to wash off his hair, and Stan followed his example. Wally had brought along a straight razor as well, and the two were able to shave off the several-days' growth of beard each had sprouted. When they had finished, and the remaining water had turned an unpleasant brownish-black, Wally pointed out towels next to a loaf of bread and a slab of cheese on a tray. The pair helped themselves to everything.

"There's a little problem," he announced as the two of them dried off, feeling cleaner than they had in centuries despite the primitive bathing conditions. "Miss Maggie asked me to loan you some of my clothes, but I only keep the one spare outfit around here."

He held up one rolled-up bundle of clothes, and the pair nodded uncertainly. Wally was at least a head shorter than either of them, and with an ample waistline.

"Who wants them?" asked Wally, holding them up with one hand.

"You mean only one of us gets any clothes?" asked Stan.

"I didn't say that," said Wally.

"Oh, okay," said a relieved Stan. "Then why don't you give those to Jack?"

"But you're shorter than I am," protested Jack.

"Yeah, but you're fatter than me," said Stan.

"Look, I don't care who wears 'em, but I don't want to stand here all day," said Wally, tossing the bundle to a frowning Jack.

"Where's my clothes?" asked Stan.

Wally picked up another bundle and handed it to Stan.

"Here you go," said Wally. "Compliments of Miss Maggie."

An alarmed Stan slowly unrolled the bundle, only to find one of Maggie's dresses and a bonnet.

"Is this supposed to be a joke?" asked the long-suffering Stan.

"Oh, yeah," sympathized Jack. "You shouldn't be wearing earth tones this time of year."

"I'll give you earth tones—"

"Please, we're doing the best we can," said Wally. "Is there anything else you need?"

The pair, who had started to dress, went silent for a moment.

"As a matter of fact, we were looking for the power—for the greenish crystal that was with the wreckage from our flying machine," said Jack. "It was kind of bright?..."

"You could even say it glowed," added Stan.

"Yeah, yeah, I know just what you're talkin' about," said Wally, walking over to the spot where he had placed it on the ground. "It was right over here..."

Wally bent over and started patting the ground.

"We already looked there," said Stan.

"No, no, I just set it down right here a few minutes ago," said Wally, becoming more concerned as he expanded the area of his search.

Jack had finished dressing, and stood there with bare arms and legs sticking out of the too-short sleeves and pants. The too-short clothing was belied by the ample mid-section and the folds of loose material that hung around his waist. Though he was more concerned with the matter at hand, he fidgeted with the sleeves and waistband as they grilled Wally.

"We already looked everywhere," said Stan.

"It's gone," said Jack.

"No, no, you don't understand," said Wally. "That's impossible. I set it right down there just before you fellas got here. The only other person who's been here—"

He paused, leaving Stan and Jack on edge.

"Who? Who?" asked Jack.

"Burt—Burt the junkman," said Wally, thinking aloud. "I almost had him haul your things away, but I told him to wait, I did."

"Where is he?" asked Jack. "What does he look like?"

Wally gave him a simple description of Burt and his pushcart, while Stan struggled with the stays on his dress.

"Where can we find him? If he's got it, we have to find him!" cried Jack.

"He was going to come back tomorrow instead—Miss Maggie didn't want me to get rid of your junk too soon. Is that thing important, that crystal?"

"Where? Where?" begged Jack.

"Don't know for sure," said Wally, shaking his head. "You might try heading over by Covent Garden—seems like he used to do a fair amount of buying and selling around there—"

But before he had finished, the two men had started off.

"Wrong way!" called Wally. "The other direction! Just past Trafalgar Square!"

The pair immediately turned around and acknowledged Wally with a friendly wave.

"Now remember where this place is so we don't get lost again," Jack said quietly.

Stan was decked out in Maggie's dress, but his walk was not particularly ladylike. The bonnet covered enough of his hair so that if he tried, he just might pass as a woman.

"I don't like this," said Stan.

"Don't worry," said Jack. "You look fetching, even if your shoes don't match your outfit. Remember, as soon as we step out of the alley, you're going to have to act more like a woman."

"What do you mean?"

"You know," said Jack. "Smaller, more demure gestures. Keep your legs closed. And stay quiet. Let me do most of the talking."

Stan hiked up his dress a bit.

"That's what got us into all this," he muttered to himself.

Sarah put the apples into her cloth bag, thanked the greengrocer and handed him a coin. She was running late and needed to get home to start dinner, but couldn't help notice the fine-looking tomatoes in the next stall. She took a step over and picked one up.

"Them's the last ones I got," said the proprietor, a plump older lady with a gap-toothed smile. "I'll do yer a deal. All I got for tuppence."

Sarah wrinkled her brow. "I wasn't really looking for tomatoes."

"Come on, ma'am," she grinned even wider, exposing more tooth decay. "Soon as I sell 'em, I can go home!"

"Tuppence? Isn't that a little high?"

"Tell you what I'll do—I'll throw in a potato—," she said, reaching into the cart behind her and searching with her hand. "Must have sold my last potatoes..."

Sarah stepped back, but the older lady held out a hand to stop her.

"Wait a minute now. I got something else..." she said, searching through a bag. "This—and the tomatoes—for tuppence."

She held up the prize she had plucked from her bag. It was a crystal as big as her fist, set inside a small metal base. She looked closer, and saw that it was glowing a soft green color, a glow emanating from deep inside the rock.

Sarah had never seen such an object. It looked oddly familiar to her, but she couldn't place it. Where had she seen it before?

"Pretty, ain't it?" she said. "Look at how bright it glows! My 'usband Burt just found it—'e's in the salvage and reclamation trade, 'e is. Almost too pretty to sell."

Suddenly, Sarah realized where she had seen it before. It was in the plans for the time machine that Sam was trying to build! What a strange coincidence. What did he call it? A power crystal?

"If I wasn't lookin' to get home now, I could probably get sixpence for just the rock! What'll it be, Ma'am?" she asked. "Last chance—take it or leave it!"

"Sam might like that," she mumbled.

Sarah hadn't meant to say it out loud, and in fact hadn't realized she had done so until the older lady responded.

"What's that, dearie?" she asked.

"My husband, Sam Warner," she answered. "He's an inventor. He'd probably like it. His workshop is about ten minutes from here."

The older lady just looked at her quizzically.

Sarah felt awkward, like she was babbling. Well, it might make a nice joke for Sam, she thought to herself, since it wasn't too expensive. Besides, she had been rather negative with him before she left home. Hadn't she said something about getting him a power crystal at the market? Sam used to complain about her sense of humor, but even he would have to admit this was funny. She smiled at the thought.

"I'm sorry," she said. "I'll take it."

Chapter Sixteen

1768

Franklin was trembling.

He had ducked into an alleyway after first making sure he wasn't followed. Nervously, he pulled from beneath his jacket his battered black notebook, filled with all of his observations and research on electricity.

Even though it was his, he felt guilty about stealing his journal back. It had been sitting on DaVinci's rolltop desk. The top had been pulled partially closed, but Franklin still recognized the worn binding and the red ribbon sewn into the spine that he used as a bookmark. When the Italian turned his back, he could not resist, and impulsively grabbed it, slipping it under his coat. He immediately regretted it, and since that moment, dozens of disastrous scenarios had flashed through his mind. What if it was a trick, a set-up, and the King's troops were following him even now? What if DaVinci had interceded for him, just gotten the notebook back, and was about to return it to him? Suppose it was the wrong notebook in the first place?

His heart was pounding as he glanced at the volume. It certainly looked similar. He opened it and began flipping through the pages, beginning at the front. His familiar handwriting and drawings were there, just as he had remembered them. They represented the culmination of his years of research into the nature of electricity and the most efficient, practical manner of harnessing its power. All of his secrets were there, waiting to reveal themselves to anyone with the knowledge and resources to implement them. Someone like...DaVinci?

As he reached his final pages, he was about to close the notebook and return it to his jacket, when he noticed something strange. He had filled up the first half of the book, but had gotten no further than that. Yet there were dozens of pages in the latter part of the volume that were filled with more writings and drawings in an unfamiliar hand. There were motors, generators, engines of all sorts that appeared to be adapted for electrical power; bombs, guns, armored vehicles, flying machines and other mechanical objects of all shapes and sizes. Most of them seemed to utilize his own theories on electricity. He looked more closely. His suspicions were confirmed when he saw that much of the handwriting was in Italian.

Franklin took a deep breath, frightened, angry, and fascinated as he studied the writings. DaVinci had taken his theories and developed practical applications, the likes of which he had not yet imagined. What did it mean? He closed the book, stuck it between his jacket and his shirt and used his upper arm to hold it tightly against his body. He peered out of the alley again, but no one appeared to be watching.

As he began walking rather quickly toward his home, he suddenly stopped short. What was he doing? He couldn't go home now! The moment the theft was discovered, everyone in town would be looking for him. And from the looks of his writings, DaVinci would be anxious to get them back. The constables were probably at his place at that moment, waiting for him to arrive. What to do?

The Near Future

Mr. Hodges looked out over the dozens of disbelieving faces before him. Standing at the podium, he could easily survey their reactions to the statement he had just delivered.

Of course, their first, logical response had been disbelief. Although time travel itself was not completely unfamiliar to the general public, most people were skeptical of the entire concept—or at least suspicious enough to avoid investing in it. And after the entire program had been co-opted by the military, the small percentage of the public that had accepted it became cynical of the whole matter, most convinced it was a hoax perpetrated by the government to cover up some military atrocity or political sex scandal.

Hodges had been a little nervous himself when he began talking. He wasn't used to public speaking in this way, and in fact, it was his first solo press conference. Though he hadn't known it at the time, it was a slow news day, which helped to account for nearly three dozen reporters and photographers, most of them somewhat prominent, and even one national anchorman. Pretty good, he thought, considering he had only decided to call the press briefing just a few hours ago.

As he spoke, offering up paperwork and citing details, he could see the reporters gradually relaxing, listening, believing—and finally becoming excited. By the time he finished with his initial statement, most of them were literally on the edges of their seats, and bursting with questions.

"Are you saying this Chronological Anomaly can't be stopped?" called the loudest of them.

"That's about the size of things," he nodded. "All of our Time Hoppers are in such a state of disrepair that it would take weeks to get one functional."

"When will this thing wipe us out?" shouted another.

"The most current research shows it hitting us between ten and ten-thirty p.m. the day after tomorrow," said a calm Hodges.

"Will everything be wiped out?" asked yet another.

"Not necessarily," he answered. "Any buildings, large plants and geological formations around since the mid-18th Century have a fairly good chance of surviving. Humans in the remotest areas who have remained untouched by Western civilization may even have a chance. Everybody else—nope."

"You mean we're all going to die?" stammered a well-known news anchorman.

"No, no. No one's going to die. We're just not going to exist anymore. One minute we'll all be walking and talking the way we always do. The next minute, we won't be here."

"Will it hurt?" said the anchorman.

Hodges swore he saw tears forming in his eyes. He was just the tiniest bit ashamed of himself for enjoying this as much as he was. "There's no way to tell, really."

"What will be here instead of us?" called another voice. The room had grown still as the import of his words sunk in.

"There's no way to tell that, either," he said. "Both worlds are pretty much unchanged until the 1760s. Whatever happened then to change the world has continued to resonate and grow. The world that evolved from that change will be the one that takes over here in our time."

"Whose fault is this, anyway?" called a betrayed-sounding voice.

"Yeah, how could this happen?" whined another.

"There really isn't any need to look for someone to blame here," said Hodges, feeling smug but keeping a straight face. "When the Army took over this project, they did everything possible to maintain the strictest control over a very challenging project."

"So it's the Army's fault?" called one.

"Who was in charge?" asked the reporter next to him.

"Let me make one thing clear: this is not the Army's fault," said Hodges sternly, though inwardly he was giddy at the ease in which he was able to point the finger at those bastards.

"Who was the officer in charge? Who can we interview to get more information?"

"I really don't know," said Hodges, "Though you may want to start with Colonel Hall. That's Lonnie Hall, L-O-N-N-I-E H-A-L-L. He was the one placed in charge when it was taken away from the private sector."

"So all this happened under his watch?"

"That's not how I would have put it..."

In the back of the room, several camera crews were scrambling out of the room and setting up in the hallway. Hodges was concerned that they were getting bored or dubious, until he caught a snatch of conversation from one of them.

"—We've still got time to go live with this—" one of the reporters ordered, and Hodges suddenly realized that, naturally, they would be in a hurry to get this story on the air.

"I'm afraid that's about all the time I have," he announced to the remaining reporters, holding his hand up and stepping back.

As they moved away, most of their fingers were frantically dialing phones or skittering across computer pads, and Hodges retreated to his office. There, he pulled a small portable monitor out of the back of a filing cabinet, then turned it to one of the news sites. There he saw the news anchorman who had been on the verge of tears less than five minutes ago, standing in the hallway in the midst of several other camera crews.

"A nationally-known scientist formerly in charge of an experimental time-traveling program says the end of the world is only two days away," he announced solemnly into the camera. "And, he has overwhelming evidence to back up his warning."

And as the anchorman unraveled the story to the rest of the country, Hodges flipped through the dial. All of the news shows were reporting from his hallway, all of the reporters equally grave.

A graphic came up behind the last reporter. In large red letters, it read "The End of the World."

1848

"Where is it, luv?" asked Burt, clutching at her arm.

The older lady turned to see her husband, an anxious look on his face, apparently flanked by a very odd-looking couple.

The man was dressed in an ill-fitting suit; his arms and legs were far too long for his coat and pants; and the woman was striking in her unattractiveness, made worse by the angry look on her face. In fact, the man appeared to be nervous and upset about something, too.

"Uh...where's what?" she asked.

"The green crystal I gave you, the big one," he asked her a bit more sharply. "What did you do with it?"

For a moment, she thought about lying but decided it wasn't appropriate. After all, she had done nothing wrong. "I sold it. That's why you gave it to me, wasn't it?"

"There's been a bit of a mix-up," said Burt. "I thought I was supposed to take it, but these folks caught up with me and told me I was wrong. They say it's from some new-fangled flying machine, and they were storing it at the Wells garage. They're cousins of the family."

"And we need it back," said Jack, slowly and clearly, his over-enunciated syllables underscoring his clothing as an indication of possibly dangerous lunacy.

"B-but I don't have it," she repeated.

"Then we have—" Stan's voice broke as Jack nudged him in the stomach. On their search for Burt, both of them realized that their current outfits made rather good disguises, and they decided to play their parts. Stan attempted a falsetto as he repeated, "Then we have to go find it."

"Where could it be, Ma'am?" asked Jack. "Do you remember who you sold it to?"

The older lady knitted her brow. Burt coaxed her with his eyes and with his words as he leaned over and whispered to her. "If we help them, they promised us a couple of shillings. If we don't—well, they may tell Specserv that I nicked the green crystal."

She turned to Stan and Jack.

"Middle-aged lady. Fairly well dressed, seen her around here before, so she probably lives nearby."

"Do you know her name?" asked Stan.

"No, no. She mentioned her husband's name. Warren? Willis? Warner? Something like that. Said he was an inventor. Yeah, that's right, said his workshop was about ten minutes away from 'ere. That's right."

"Ten minutes away!" said Jack to Stan. "How hard can it be to find her?"

"I don't know..." said Stan. "How many people are living in London?"

Jack turned to the older lady. "Which way did she go?"

"Over there," she pointed. "May've going home. Had a bag of tomatoes. Likely going to fix dinner for her family. That's right. Mrs. Chapman said she had eight or nine children. What was her name?..."

"Mrs. Chapman?" asked a puzzled Stan.

"No—Warner! That was it, Sam Warner! That's the name!"

"Great!" said Jack, clapping his hands together and grinning. "Tell Maggie Wells that Jack said to give you a shilling. No, make it two shillings!"

And the odd-looking couple slipped away, heading in the direction the older lady had pointed, confident that they would soon be going home.

The Near Future

"I told you once, Colonel," said a rather uncomfortable Hodges. "I was never told not to speak to the press. Besides, the people have a right to know. What harm can it do?"

"What harm can it do? Is that what you're asking me? What harm can it do?" asked the Colonel.

Hodges rolled his eyes.

"I'll tell you what harm it can do, Mister!" ranted the Colonel, obviously relishing the opportunity to berate the stupid civilian.

He was interrupted by the sound of squealing tires and a crash in the distance.

"Did you hear that?" asked the Colonel, suddenly excited. "Come over here!"

He half-dragged Hodges over to the window. There, in the street below, two cars had collided in an intersection. The drivers were out of their cars, obviously agitated, screaming in each other's faces.

All around them, the scene was chaotic. Looting was rampant, and people of all shapes, sizes and ages were running through the streets with their arms full of goods. Older people were apparently hoarding groceries, younger ones were lumbering along boldly carrying TVs and stereos.

"Look at that! And it's all thanks to you," snapped the Colonel. "Do you know what that is? Do you know what I'm seeing? I'm seeing the complete breakdown of our entire goddam social order, that's what!"

"Looks like a bunch of idiots to me," mumbled Hodges.

"What? What are you talking about?"

"Not my fault. They didn't hear me," said Hodges. "If they had, they'd know that all the cases of Spam and pork and beans and Blu-Ray players and flatscreens aren't going to do them the slightest bit of good when this thing all comes down. No, that's just a bunch of idiots panicking down there."

"And don't you think that the end of the world as we know it is a pretty goddam good reason to panic?"

Hodges started toward the door, but the Colonel grabbed his arm to stop him.

"And where do you think you're going?"

"I have things to do, Colonel."

"More interviews, maybe? Forget it! You're not going anywhere, Mister. Consider yourself under house arrest!"

"Are you crazy? You can't do this!"

"It's done. Because of your little press conference, we're all under martial law!" barked the Colonel.

"Oh, that's just great! That's really going to accomplish a lot."

"Haven't you accomplished enough already on your own?"

"Colonel, I think you'd at least better give me access to the tracking equipment."

"Now that's about the last place you'll be going!" laughed the Colonel derisively. "You won't be getting any nearer to the monitoring station than the stockade."

"Are you crazy?" choked Hodges. "Colonel, I think you'd better have someone near that equipment that knows how to use it!"

"Don't you worry your little egghead about that," sniffed the Colonel. "We've got the finest brains in the Army studying that equipment of yours."

"They're not—they're not—touching anything—are they?" said Hodges, truly starting to panic.

"How the hell else are they gonna figure out how to work it?"

"But those men may still be trying to return! What is going on here, Colonel?"

"I suppose I can tell you, since you're not going anywhere. The Army is about to pull your fat out of the fire, son."

Hodges started to quiver, and took a seat.

"They're not—"

"You betcha. The Army's gonna build one of its own Time Hoppers. We're sending our own people into the past to straighten out this whole goddam mess."

"No—you don't understand—"

The Colonel looked at him, uncomprehending.

"You have to keep that equipment just the way it is, Colonel. Please! If that equipment is disturbed, even if the timenauts try to return to the present day, they won't be able to! They'll be stuck in the past for good—and that means all of us are goners!"

"And you think you know more about all this than the United States Army?" said the Colonel accusingly.

"All the Army knows about this whole business is what I've told them!" insisted Hodges. "There's still a chance those two timenauts can go back and repair the damage before our whole timeline is irrevocably changed—if we let them! But if we destroy their beacon—"

"What the hell are you talking about, Mister?" asked the Colonel disdainfully.

"Okay, suppose those two were in a ship just off the coast," said Hodges slowly. "As long as we keep the lighthouse going, there's still a chance they can see it and we can guide them safely to shore. But now, the Army is trying to tear the lighthouse down and build a ship out of it to go rescue them!"

"That would be the Navy, son."

"Army, Navy, who cares?" ranted Hodges. "They're going to destroy the only chance those two have of getting home. And if they can't get home, then that's it—the timeline is automatically corrupted and we're all goners!"

"Oh yeah?" The Colonel squinted and looked balefully at the frantic Hodges. "Well, when that happens, you can bet the U.S. Army will be having the last laugh!"

Chapter Seventeen

1768

Leonardo DaVinci's apartment was a shambles. Books and papers were strewn across the floor, drawers were yanked open, furniture was pulled out of place and cushions sitting where they had been thrown hours before. When he had tired of searching his study and his bedroom, the hunt had been carried over to the kitchen, where all of the cupboards and drawers were emptied of utensils, food, and knick-knacks. Many people would be amazed to learn the Old Man had accumulated this much mess in only seven short years, but right now untidiness was the last thing on his mind.

The Italian stood in the middle of the disarray, wringing his hands helplessly. Where could it be? As he had exhausted every other possibility, he was slowly coming to the realization that Franklin must have pilfered his notebook. He had been so busy trying to jam incriminating documents into the American's pocket that he had completely forgotten to hide the notebook with all of his electrical theories.

Damn! How could he do that? thought DaVinci. Admittedly, it was Franklin's own notebook, and he was simply stealing it back. But now? The timing could simply not have been worse. Lord North was expecting him to discuss his latest inventions, needed to quash the uprising in the Far East.

Worse yet, the soldiers had not yet returned to inform him of the arrest of Franklin for possessing incriminating documents. *How can that be?* wondered DaVinci. *I know they're there. I put them there!*

The Old Man had made a deal. He was supposed to frame Franklin with the incriminating plans. The British soldiers were then to arrest the American and report back to him afterward, so he would have the honor of informing Lord North and His Majesty. It was perfectly simple! But he hadn't heard back from them. Could they have cocked it up somehow?

And now his notebook was missing, just before his big meeting with North. Did Franklin suspect something? Is that why he stole back his own notebook?

DaVinci was pacing now, back and forth between his desk and the front door. If he didn't leave now, he would be late. He would have to do without his notes. He could discuss the weaponry design with no problem, but the electrical power packs would be quite a different matter. However, Lord North made it none too easy to think on his feet at even the simplest meeting—and nothing about this meeting would be simple. The British were facing a crisis in India, and wanted to begin a campaign of terror that would crush all thoughts of resistance—even if it did take the lives of a few thousand natives.

There was a knock on his front door.

"Yes, what is it?" he asked impatiently, throwing open his chamber door to see the unflappable Jameson.

"Your meeting, sir," he said. "You're going to be late."

Jameson held his cloak and hat in his arms. A good and faithful servant, that Jameson; he wouldn't have lasted long in the eighteenth century without him.

"You are correct as always, Jameson," said DaVinci, as his servant placed the cloak across his shoulders. "Thank you."

"Very good, sir," said Jameson. "And will you be requiring anything else?"

DaVinci stopped for a moment.

"You didn't happen to hear anything about Dr. Franklin, did you Jameson?" he asked.

"Sir?" said an uncomprehending Jameson.

"Nothing involving the authorities?" he asked.

Jameson shook his head no.

"I see. Thank you."

And DaVinci walked out the door, dreading the meeting ahead.

The carriage was still recognizable, but just barely. Bonomi circled around it slowly, hands on his hips, studying the modifications but still keeping a respectful distance. Every now and again, he would give out a low whistle whenever he saw a feature that he found particularly interesting.

Sam stood in a corner by a workbench, watching his reactions. It was the first time he had shown the Time Carriage to anyone besides Sarah, and he was quite interested in gauging his reaction. Granted, it was only Bonomi, but if he was impressed, there was a good chance his investors would be, too.

The carriage and its assorted parts took up most of the coach house, and Bonomi had to step over several bits of debris on the ground. When he had almost come full circle, he stopped and let out with his lowest, longest whistle yet.

"What are you looking at?" asked Sam.

"Look at this!" Bonomi marveled. "I don't know if it does anything, but it looks beautiful!"

Sam followed his gaze to the power crystal, now mounted in place.

"That's the power crystal," explained Sam, and grabbed the plans to show him where it was included in the original drawings. "See, it goes right in here, just behind—"

"Is it really glowing?" asked Bonomi, sounding like an overeager kid. "Look! It's green! What does it do?"

"According to the plans—I mean, it provides the power for the whole operation," said Sam.

"Where did you get it?"

"My wife picked it up at the market," said Sam.

"No, no, seriously," said Bonomi.

"Oh, yes, seriously," said Sam. "Well, it was very difficult to—to develop and infuse it with enough power to—operate the drive."

"I hope it works as good as it looks," said Bonomi.

"Oh, it will," said Sam.

Sam hoped he sounded more confident than he felt. When Sarah brought home a crystal that looked exactly like the one in the schematics, he couldn't resist wiring it in place. If he didn't know better, he'd say it was the real thing, and even glowed a faint green color. There was a slot in the bottom of the base that seemed to accommodate all of the wires, and he hooked it up according to the plans. It was almost like it belonged there. God only knew how Sarah managed to get her hands on it, but he saw little need to question his good fortune at the moment.

The Time Carriage was coming along nicely. Sam had constructed it according to the plans, but unfortunately, he seemed to have reached his limit. Nineteenth Century technology in this timeline had permitted him to accomplish a great deal structurally while keeping faithful to those plans. If he completed the rest of it—with the proper materials—for all he knew, it might actually work. The problem was that he was missing a few key components—the "energizer," the "gyrogear," the "stabilizer." None of which he had ever heard of outside of his dubious drawings, and none of which likely existed in the first place. He hoped the work he had done thus far would be enough for Bonomi to obtain more funding from his financiers. Either way, he would undoubtedly have to find a stabilizer, even if he had to carve it out of wood and paint it to look like the object in the drawings.

Bonomi's reaction was very encouraging, and he hoped that would carry over to the people who held the purse strings.

"So, Sam, how much more have you got to go?" asked Bonomi.

"Oh, not too much, really," he answered.

Sam reached for the closest set of plans and held them up for Bonomi to point out the various components.

"We need to add the gyrogear here, and then the stabilizer will go right there," he said.

"Any problem completing them?"

"Not really, sir, not as long as the funding continues. I'm going to need to have the glass cover made here, and these pointed things on the end are pure silver. They won't be cheap, but we want it to work now, don't we?" asked Sam, trying to sound confident and convincing.

"Excuse me, Sam?" came a voice from the doorway. "These two—people—insisted on speaking with you."

He turned to see a rather disheveled-looking Jack and a less than perfectly coiffed Stan, whose scarf and bonnet seemed to be battling it out with each other. Sam noticed that their eyes were riveted to the carriage, despite its unfinished state, and the pair slowly approached it, oblivious to anyone or anything else in the coach house.

"I'm afraid this isn't a very convenient time, Mister—? Miss—?" Sam let the questions dangle in the air, unanswered. Sarah knew that no one was to be allowed back here, he thought, so what—and why—were these two doing staring at his would-be time machine? And was that a flicker of recognition in their eyes? Sam was feeling angry and uncomfortable at this intrusion, but was simply too curious to just throw them out.

"It almost looks like Nellie..." murmured the man in the ill-fitting suit to the woman, just loud enough for Sam to overhear.

Nellie? Who the devil was Nellie? wondered Sam.

"I did try to talk them out of it, but I'm afraid they insisted," said Sarah sharply. "They knew about the package I got at the market."

"There it is!" cried the woman. At least she was dressed like a woman—she certainly didn't sound like one. She was pointing to the power crystal. "It's still got a little juice left."

They know about the power crystal? This could either be really, really good, or really, really bad. "Excuse me—" he interjected.

"Sam, may I speak with you for a moment?" said Bonomi in a voice that let Sam know there was no alternative. Sam followed him over to the far corner, where Bonomi addressed him in a low, confidential tone.

"If you're trying to drag in a couple of other investors—" warned Bonomi.

"No, no sir, nothing like that at all," said Sam, trying to pacify him.

"Look, I'll get you the money if I have to beg for it!" said Bonomi. "But you're not going to let anyone else in on this!"

"All right, that's fine," said Sam, almost too stunned to recognize the shifting balance of power.

"I mean it, Sam! I need to go now if I'm going to have your money by tomorrow, but I'll have it, by God!" cursed the Italian. "Now don't forget, we have a deal!"

"Uh—right, sir!" said Sam, as Bonomi stormed toward the door, brushing past Sarah and making his way to the center of London.

It couldn't have worked out better if he had planned it that way, thought Sam, smiling. If nothing else, he'd definitely be getting some money to tide them over. When he glanced over at the strange couple, he quickly stopped smiling.

"Get away from that!" shouted Sarah at the pair.

The two of them were crowded around the power crystal, and the woman appeared to be tugging on it.

"Stop that! Stop it now!" cried Sam, running over to them. "What are you doing?"

"I just told you, this is our power crystal!" said the man.

"The devil it is!" warned Sam. "Leave it alone!"

"That's right!" said Sarah. "I bought it fair and square, off that old lady in Covent Garden!"

"Well then, you were buying stolen property!" said Stan, trying to retain his falsetto and his bonnet.

"That's right, it's stolen property! And if you don't let us alone, we'll call the police! And I bet you don't want them to see what you're working on!" said Jack, playing a hunch.

At that last statement, Sam stopped short. No, it would not do at all for Specserv to see him building a fraudulent "Time Carriage" in his coach house.

But Sarah wasn't cowed by his threat. She tried one more time to pull the woman away from the power crystal. Stan didn't budge, but when he pushed her back, she clung tight to his bonnet and scarf.

When she regained her composure, Sarah looked over to see a man in a dress, fidgeting and looking uncomfortable.

The sight of Stan revealed instilled in Sam a bit of bravado. This time, he recognized the shift in the balance of power immediately. He swaggered over to Stan, looked him up and down and then stared him in the face.

"So you're going to call the police on us?" he questioned. "And what is it you're going to tell them? That we stole your power crystal, Miss—? Oh, I'm sorry, Mister—?"

"Sam, why do I get the feeling that they've got more secrets than we do?" asked a smiling Sarah.

"Now wait a minute—" said Stan, confused and still speaking in a falsetto.

"Wait, let's be reasonable," said Jack. "What are the two of you going to do with a power crystal? You don't even know what it's used for!"

Suddenly Jack caught sight of the tools, the plans on the workbench—and the NLE-13 Operator's Manual. He let out an audible gasp.

"That power crystal is worth a lot to us!" said Sarah.

"The Operator's Manual! You've got it! Of course!" cried Jack, picking up the weather-beaten booklet and cradling it in his arms like an infant.

Stan began giggling nervously.

"We can go home!" he said.

"Why do you want—" asked Sam, stopping in mid-sentence as the implications of Stan's last statement started sinking in. *We can go home? If this time machine really works, then where could they mean by "home?" If this really was their book, their plans—could it be?*

Sam looked at the pair more closely. The man was dressed in a nondescript suit, but the sleeves of his jacket were several inches above his wrist, and the shirt and waistline appeared baggy. The trousers were very tight, and ended just past the midway point of his calves, so that several inches of his bare white skin was exposed. *That would explain his manner of dress. It's what futuristic fashions would be like!* thought Sam.

He glanced over at the man in woman's clothing, and without thinking raised a worried eyebrow. Was this sort of thing typical of the future? He winced and decided he was glad to be living in the present day.

Sarah appeared confused. While she was quite bright for a woman, thought Sam, she was completely unprepared to embrace the complexities of time travel.

"You'd best put that book down!" she warned Jack. "It's nothing to do with you! It used to belong to my husband's grandfather."

"Of course!" said Jack to Stan. "It's been here all this time, with this family! They may have even gotten it from DaVinci!"

"Wait a minute," said Sam cautiously. "Are you saying that book was written by Leonardo DaVinci?"

"No, no, not written by," said Stan. "We brought it from home. He picked it up after he fell out of our time machine. You see, we were—"

Jack immediately nudged him in the ribs so hard that it took his breath away.

"What my friend means to say is—um—" explained Jack.

"Where do you two come from—really?" asked Sam, accusingly.

Jack shot a silent glance at Stan that warned him to keep quiet.

"That's a good question," stammered Jack. "Uh—we're—Americans. That's right, Americans."

"All right, then when do you come from?" asked Sarah sharply.

Sam looked up, surprised at her directness. Before they could answer, she continued her interrogation.

"We've got the book, and it says in the front that it was printed 200 years from now. My husband knows all about it, so don't lie to us," she continued.

"It really works!" gasped Sam. "By God, the thing really works!"

Jack looked at Stan and sighed. The jig appeared to be up. Sarah suddenly stepped up and snatched the manual from Jack's arms and stepped over to the fireplace. Although it wasn't lit at the moment, it gave her words added weight.

"If you don't tell us the truth, you'll never see the power crystal or the book again!" Sarah threatened.

"No, no!" cried Stan.

"Wait, wait, we'll tell you!" said Jack trying to ease the situation. "Calm down, please! I'll tell you the whole story. You see—"

"You—you two are really from the future!" said Sam. He spoke very slowly, cutting off Jack and giving voice to the inconceivable thoughts that he was being forced to accept. "The time machine really works. This is your book. You—you must have lost it while you were traveling in the past, and you've been looking for it all this time. For some reason—I don't know, maybe you're having some kind of mechanical trouble—but you need it so you can get back to your home in the future. You tracked it down here and you want to use it— and the power crystal—to fix your own time machine."

Jack stood there with his mouth open, occasionally nodding slowly, as Sam's uncannily accurate assessment of their situation continued. When his voice trailed off, Jack tried to think of something to add, but couldn't in the moments of silence that followed. An astonished Stan was the first to speak.

"That's right!" he said.

"So what do we do now?" asked Jack.

"Look," said Sam. "This is a very unusual situation. I guess the power crystal and the book really do belong to you. They really are more important to you than they are to me—"

"Sam!" gasped Sarah.

"Let me finish, please," said Sam, and turned to Stan and Jack. "I suppose I really wouldn't feel right about keeping them, even though I've put a lot of time and money into this. But, I'll find some way to put food on the table for Sarah and myself and the nine children. The plans are on the workbench, and I'll help you remove the power crystal from the carriage. I guess you'd better take them with you."

"Look, we're only doing this because we have no choice, you know," said Jack. "We have to get home, we really do. It's going to be hard enough with the manual and the crystal, but without them, we'll never get back. We're not a couple of jerks. I hope you can understand."

"I mean, you don't even have a chronostat," said Stan. "The only reason you finished as much as you did is because you got hold of a power crystal."

Sam nodded sadly. There it was, then, all down the drain. Everything was lost. He'd probably have to give back the money Bonomi had given him up to this point, and he didn't have a shilling. He'd be lucky if he wasn't arrested.

"It's all right," said Sam quietly.

The two men from the future turned to the nearest workbench and started picking up the plans.

"Just a minute," said Sarah.

They stopped and turned around to face her, eyebrows raised. Sam was also puzzled, but said nothing.

"You two are going to go back to your time machine now, is that right?" asked Sarah. "And you're going to try to fix it?"

"Uh—yes," said Jack, with the feeling of someone being led into a trap.

"And you're leaving us here," she continued. "Leaving us with a perfectly good time machine that's only missing a power crystal and a stabilizer, and a couple of other little things. Little things that are probably hanging off the wreckage that you're going to go back and try to fix, even though it's going to take you forever."

"I don't follow you," said Stan.

"And my Sam here is going to be left with his own time machine, which is almost finished, except he's never going to be able to complete it because he's missing just a very few parts," said Sarah. "Parts that only you two can provide for him."

"Keep talking," said Sam.

"Think about it," said Sarah. "In my own opinion, the three of you could accomplish a whole lot more working together than you can separately."

Jack was silent and thoughtful. She was starting to make sense, all right.

"My husband is a brilliant man," she implored. "He's an inventor. He's very smart. He can fix it for you, I know he can! Look what he's been able to do so far, just working on his own. He read all of your plans, adapted them to the tools he has at hand, and built a full size replica. Just imagine what he could accomplish with your help. He could solve all of your problems."

"And in return?" asked Jack.

"Not awfully much, really," said Sarah. "I'm sure he and his chief investor would want to take a journey or two in it when it is completed, if only to prove to his investor that he can do what he says he can. Perhaps a bit of compensation for all of his work. Whatever seems fair."

Stan and Jack looked at each other.

"We—have a mission to accomplish before we go home," said Jack.

"Yeah, we have to fix this problem," said Stan. "When we were traveling here, we picked up—"

"Now, now," said Jack. "We don't need to bother them with our problems. My point is, we need a time machine for our mission, and to get back to our own time. If you can guarantee us that, then we will be glad to work with you."

"Then we have a deal," said Sam.

He held his hand out cautiously.

"Do men still shake hands in the future?" he asked.

Chapter Eighteen

The Near Future

Corporal Frank Spumoni sat in what was now the Briefing Room. He was not sure why he had been chosen for what was being presented to him as an "honor," and he was not particularly pleased to be chosen. Still, he knew he should feign enthusiasm at his selection.

Men in suits and army brass circulated around the room. Several of them were familiar faces around the command center, while others he had never seen before. When they were anywhere within earshot of him, however, they spoke to one another in suspiciously low voices.

Frank strained to hear them, but could only catch a few brief snatches of conversation. What he heard did not allay his fears. He overheard phrases like "spin control," "acceptable risk," "cover our asses," and "trained monkey."

Every few minutes, one of the suits—usually carrying a clipboard—would walk over to him and ask him a few vague questions.

"So, how are you feeling, son?"

"Fine, sir," he would answer.

"Are you excited about the mission?"

"Oh, yes, sir, very excited," he would answer.

"Good, good," they would respond, and then walk away. He assumed this was their attempt to fraternize with him. He hoped their motives were altruistic, but he feared that it was more likely so that after he died while serving his country on this high-profile mission, they would be able to tell the national press: "Yes, yes, I knew that boy well. We had lots of long talks together, Frank and I. A brave man and a credit to his uniform. Served his country well. I'm going to miss him." And then sell the story of their friendship with the late young hero Frank Spumoni to the highest bidder.

Everything had erupted after Mr. Hodges held his press conference. All hell had broken loose, and the military and the politicians decided some damage control was necessary. Their plan involved a very public rescue mission with a hero plucked from the ranks of the Army. And so, once again in his military career, Corporal Spumoni had been plucked by the Army.

Of course, Hodges had gotten most of it right in his press conference, but what he didn't realize was that the Army actually had begun to reconstruct its own Time Hopper. Privately, the top brass considered it to be a salvage mission—they were hoping to salvage what was left of their reputations from the budding public relations apocalypse. The best brains the military could assemble began inspecting the junked remains of the previous Time Hoppers to see what they could possible dismantle and re-assemble. The feeling was that with the wreckage of five Time Hoppers to choose from, they should be able to re-assemble at least one working craft.

And what they did manage to put together indeed bore a strong resemblance to a real working Time Hopper. All the pieces were in place, the best components they could dismantle from the ruins reassembled in what looked to be the correct order. Whether they were connected correctly was a question no one seemed awfully concerned with. The biggest problem was that no one had the slightest idea where—or when—to find the missing timenauts, but that seemed to be a problem they would eagerly delegate to someone further down the chain of command. Much further.

With a Time Hopper in their hands, the next step was to find someone to pilot it into the past, to be a one-man rescue mission, find the timenauts, repair the damage to the time continuum, and especially to serve as a lightning rod to deflect criticisms of the Army.

The selection process to find their hero was quick and simple, not surprising considering the time constraints the situation had placed on them. Frank had been working right under their noses the whole time, and when Colonel Hall came up with the sudden idea to send him, it was roundly and immediately applauded.

The whole idea made Frank very nervous. If they considered this a safe mission likely to result in much glory for the chief participant, they would not be sending him. No, Frank was the sort of person who would be sent because he was considered anonymous, expendable, and not likely to be missed if he didn't return. Cannon fodder.

In two minutes, he was to be briefed on the operation of the new Time Hopper and his upcoming mission. Ten minutes later, he was scheduled for his very own press conference. That would be followed by a brief meet-and-greet session with several prominent Republican Party contributors. After that, ready or not, Frank would be sent off into the Mists of Time. And there was no doubt about it, Frank was not ready.

Several of the brass huddled in one corner of the room, talking with each other and occasionally stealing a glance toward Frank. The Corporal spotted General Dunavan, and saw that there was a second General whom he did not recognize. They seemed to be disagreeing about something, and Frank could guess what it was. Finally, a Colonel in the middle of the discussion threw up his arms and walked away, followed closely by one of the suits. Another one of the suits walked over to Frank, accompanied by the General whom he did not recognize.

When they got close, Frank immediately sprang to his feet. He was uncomfortable being around any Brass in a more informal situation, let alone a full-fledged General in crisis mode, and was not completely sure how to react. He wasn't sure whether to salute, shake hands, or bow and scrape.

"At ease, Corporal," grinned the Suit, thrusting his hand forward. Frank met it with a firm handshake, and then shook the General's hand, which was likewise extended.

"I'm General Byrd, son," said the officer. "I'm mighty pleased to meet you. Young men like you are the backbone of the Army."

"Yes, sir. Thank you, sir," said Frank.

"Just call me Crawford," said the Suit.

"Yessir, Mr.— Yessir, Crawford," said Frank.

"*Mister* Crawford," corrected the Suit.

"Frank, we'd like you to step into the next room for a few minutes," said Crawford. "We want to bring you up to speed on your mission and make sure you're clear on the operation of the craft. The press has pretty well set up, and I want to make sure you know the drill before you speak to them."

The two men ushered Frank into the adjacent room. There in the center of the room sat the reconstituted, renovated and otherwise restored NLE-X Time Hopper. To look at it did not instill confidence, thought Frank. It was tarnished and dented, and the colors on the framework did not match each other. Some of the wires were apparently being held together with black duct tape. He hoped this was not the machine he would be expected to fly solo into the past.

Scattered around the room were a variety of parts from the Time Hoppers that had been dismantled to supply parts to the one resurrected machine. There were materials and sections from at least a half dozen Time Hoppers scattered around the room, and they had to step over the pieces as they proceeded inside.

"They're just checking a couple of things before you take off," said Crawford. "So, what do you think of her?"

Frank didn't dare tell him what he really thought. The whole thing was sitting up on four concrete blocks, like a stripped-down Chevy in a trailer park. There was an occasional loose wire sticking out from the chassis, and an electrician's lamp was lying beneath it on the floor, with a black cord leading to an outlet in the wall.

"Uh...is it finished?" asked Frank.

"Is it finished? Now what the hell kind of a question is that?" asked General Byrd.

"Sorry, sir,' said Frank.

"Of course it's finished," said Crawford. "There's just a few last-minute details, that's all. You don't want to take off in it unless it's perfect, do you?"

"No, no," said Frank.

"What's the matter?" asked General Byrd. "It's the blocks, isn't it? I knew they should have taken it down off the blocks. Look, they just needed to crawl under there and have one last look at the undercarriage. But now, it's all been checked out and it's ready to go."

"Yes, sir," said Frank.

"Climb on in and have a seat," said Crawford with a proud grin. "Strap yourself in and we'll run through the commands."

"Crawford here supervised the reconstruction," said General Byrd. "He's the only person in the world who knows how to operate it."

Then why isn't Crawford flying it? wondered the Corporal to himself.

"We made a few modifications," said Crawford, with a knowing wink.

Frank climbed into the left-hand seat. He noticed a large rip in the imitation leather upholstery on the other side, and the foam padding was starting to work its way through, despite a length of silver duct tape that had at one time been placed along the length of the tear.

He reached around and grabbed the seat belt and shoulder harness, pulling them tight in front of him and adjusting them carefully. In theory, none of the Time Hoppers was supposed to engage unless the harnesses were fastened. In actual fact, many of the timenauts did not bother with the seat belts; they would fasten the buckles in place, and then use a knife or large pair of scissors to slice through the canvas straps. The buckle would be left in place in order to circumvent the safety feature, without inconveniencing the time travelers. The upshot was that this was the only remaining 'hopper seat belt system that had not been sliced, and Crawford was hoping the Corporal would appreciate the fact.

There wasn't much legroom, and so Frank had to shift in his seat in order to squeeze his knees below the instrument panel. He looked around for something to do with his hands, but nothing came to mind. There was no steering wheel, no gearshift lever, nothing to really hold on to and give him at least some illusion of control.

"Take a look around," said Crawford. "Looks just like the other ones, doesn't it?"

General Byrd said nothing, but stood there, beaming.

Frank nodded. He surveyed the bank of buttons, switches, levers, touchscreens, displays and readouts on the instrument panel in front of him. There was a keyboard, apparently for typing in commands or coordinates, and a small LED screen above it. It all looked the same, except for a few controls to his left, located slightly beneath the dash.

"Now listen up," said Crawford. "I'm going to give you the 911 on how to operate this baby."

Did he just say 911? Frank hoped that was ignorance, rather than a Freudian slip. From the few minutes he had known Crawford, he decided that he was probably safe.

"Your NLE is fully armed, fully loaded, ready to dispatch any hostiles," said Crawford.

"Uh, sir?" asked Frank. "I'm a little confused. I thought we weren't supposed to interfere with the timeline at all."

"Well, technically, no," said Crawford.

"That was our former directive, yes," said General Byrd. "But you can see how much good it did us. The fact is, if these last two timenauts had gone back fully prepared—fully able to defend themselves against hostile operatives—none of this may have happened."

Frank wondered how that could be, but saw not advantage to challenging him on it.

"We want to send you back ready to lock and load at the first sign of trouble," he continued. "And remember, if you encounter any problems at all, shoot to kill. At this point, what harm can it do?"

Frank vacillated, but tried not to let it show. This did not sound like a careful, well-thought-out plan, but he figured he was going to have to obey orders.

"To launch the ignition sequence, throw the switch on the left and press this series of buttons," said Crawford, demonstrating the correct sequence.

Several lights on the board lit up in red and yellow.

"Next, initiate the energizer." He pushed another button, and a brief sputtering was followed by a chugging sound. Frank thought it sounded familiar, not unlike the small gasoline-powered engines on the lawnmowers he used to push as a boy.

"Lock in stabilizer right over here, so you don't fly off into God knows where," Crawford said as he pressed a few numbers on the keypad and entered them. "I've just programmed it, so all you'll need to do is hit the Default setting if you have any trouble."

"Default, yes sir," said Frank.

"This toggle switch here will start up your gyrogear," said Crawford, giving it a flick with his index finger. Frank heard a low whooshing sound from beneath his seat.

"This may be a little small to transport the two timenauts and yourself back to the present, so we've added another brand-new feature," said Crawford. "This lever here will expand the field for the time portal up to an eight-foot radius beyond your principal structure. Oh, it only works on living beings. Be very careful with it."

Frank was relieved. He didn't know how he was going to transport two men if the situation arose, and he was uncomfortable with one of them sitting on his lap. But suddenly the implications of that feature struck him.

"Sir, can I ask you something?" said Frank. "If they aren't strapped in, how do we know they won't get hurt during the time hop?"

"Oh, um..." said Crawford slowly. The thought had obviously not occurred to him. "There is, of course, a minimal risk, you understand. You see, our number one priority is to recover the two timenauts before more damage is done to the Time Stream. The condition of the timenauts is a—secondary consideration. Do you understand, Corporal?"

"Yes sir." Frank understood. His message was loud and clear. Bring back the timenauts, dead or alive.

"To chart a destination, you push this, and you can enter the exact latitude and longitude," said Crawford, demonstrating. "We've even added a more basic analog feature. Press this—"

As he demonstrated, a map of the world came into view. A small crosshair sight appeared, which he aimed over Scotland. He kept pushing buttons and more detailed screens appeared, until finally he was able to place it in St. Andrews.

"This should help you even if you don't know the exact coordinates. And then, to enter the date and time you wish to appear, you just push this, and where it says 'Enter Date and Time,' you type them in," said Crawford.

"Amazing, sir!" said Frank, typing in 1764 London.

"That's pretty much it, son, 'cept for this over here," said Crawford. He leaned over to the opposite side and reached under the console, beneath the instrument panel. There was a small button with a clear plastic cover that fit loosely over it. He lifted up the plastic bubble to reveal the red button that stuck out about a half inch.

"See this button?" he asked.

Frank nodded once.

"This is only to be pressed in the greatest of emergencies," said Crawford, "only when you are faced with insurmountable odds."

"I'm afraid I don't follow you, sir," said Frank.

Crawford attempted to replace the plastic cover, but the spring, which looked like it was no larger or sturdier than the type found in most fountain pens, failed to respond. The bubble hung there, limp, exposing the button to an accidental finger or knee. Crawford made another perfunctory attempt to replace it, then gave up and hoped the Corporal wouldn't say anything embarrassing.

"This machine cannot be captured by hostiles during your journey," he continued. "No one else is to have access to this machine unless they are accompanied by you. If it appears as though you have been outnumbered, overwhelmed or otherwise surprised by native forces, then you are to reach under here, lift the plastic sheath, and press the button."

"And that will somehow immobilize the—hostile forces?" asked Frank.

"Better than that," said Crawford. "It will render the NLE completely useless to them."

Crawford smiled coldly and turned to General Byrd.

"And how will it do that, sir?" asked Frank.

"What's that, Corporal?" asked Crawford, turning his head back toward Frank, apparently trying to discourage a conversation from developing.

"I say, how will pushing the button render the NLE completely useless to them?" asked the increasingly concerned Frank.

"When you push the button, then ten seconds later, the entire thing self-destructs," Crawford said. His tone was that of someone suddenly made aware that the person he was talking with might just possibly be an idiot.

"This is a self-destruct button?" said Frank, as it slowly sank in.

"Correct, son," said Crawford.

"I hope that doesn't upset you, Corporal," said General Byrd.

"Yes—I mean no—uh—so that means if I push the self-destruct button, I would be blown up too?" he asked.

"Correct. You and everybody within a ten-foot radius, son," said Crawford with a *how 'bout that* smile. "Don't worry, though. It's only to be used as a last resort."

The moment I used it, it would automatically become the last resort, even if it hadn't been up until the moment I pushed it, reasoned Frank to himself.

"Does that bother you, son?" asked the General.

"No, not really sir," said Frank. "I guess that's because I'm not planning on having any emergencies."

"You found a good man for me, Hank," Crawford said to the General.

"He's Army, isn't he?" asked the General smugly. He looked admiringly at the slapdash paint job on the body of the Time Hopper, much as he admired the paint job on his '66 Mustang Convertible. He gathered up a corner of his jacket and wiped a tiny smudge.

"Okay, now let me show you how to finish up the launch sequence," said Crawford, turning back to Frank.

The NLE was chugging away, and Frank found he needed to listen very closely to hear the man's words.

"You can obviously tell that your energizer has been engaged," he said. "The stabilizer has been locked on, and your gyrogear has been initiated."

"Uh huh," said Frank.

"If this were a real hop, you would punch in your coordinates, the place and time for your destination," he continued.

Frank nodded.

"She's a real beauty," noted the General, apropos of nothing. He pulled out his handkerchief and leaned inside to wipe down the control panel. "You'll want to keep 'er clean."

"Then, if you were actually going to leave now, you would just need to lean over and push this button here," said Crawford, pointing to a small green button.

Unfortunately, the NLE made enough noise to impair Frank's hearing, and several things happened in very short order. As he didn't hear the first part of Crawford's previous sentence, Frank leaned over to the small green button.

When Crawford saw that Frank's finger was indeed approaching the final button, he cried "No!" and tried to dive inside to prevent Frank's finger from carrying out what he thought was an order.

Although Frank remained strapped into place, Crawford's weight forced his legs to the right and under the instrument panel. His finger was resting against the green button, while all worries about the red button were forgotten. In no time at all, his right knee snapped off the plastic sheath, which had been dangling there uselessly. Crawford's weight forced it over just a quarter of an inch more, so it rested against the red button.

And then, Crawford, off balance, reached out and found the only thing large enough to push off against. And unfortunately, when he pushed up and away from the Time Hopper, he pushed the oblivious General Byrd onto Frank's lap, moving his right knee the final fraction of an inch.

Chapter Nineteen

The Near Future

General Dunavan wore a grim, determined smile. "So there's no doubt in your mind that your team can handle it?"

Colonel Hall nodded, thinking how well he would come across on TV. He was scheduled to take a leading role in the upcoming press conference, and wondered if he would have enough time to email some of his old West Point classmates. Perhaps he would have his wife do it. After all, he did want to look humble.

"I have every confidence in Corporal Spumoni and the rest of my men," said Colonel Hall.

"Good," said the General. "We can't have another public relations disaster now, can we?"

"No sir," said Colonel Hall. "Let me put your mind at ease about that."

The General's demeanor suddenly changed. He grinned and let himself relax. The situation was obviously well in hand.

"Let me ask you, Lonnie, is that steak house still open? The place we went to last summer?" he asked.

"Oh, yes, the place next to that gentleman's club?" asked Colonel Hall. "That was quite a night! Say, why don't we—"

His next words were drowned out by the sound of the explosion from the next room. The wall shook, and the officers and the suits grew silent. After a moment, a voice muttered from the crowd "Good God! What the hell was that?" Of course, their ears were all ringing from the blast, and none of them could hear a word of it.

Colonel Hall rushed to the door and pulled it open. It separated from the frame and came off the hinges, so that he was left holding the door in the air by the knob. He held it out to his side, just inside the room, and placed it on the floor.

The others crowded around him and peered over his shoulder into the room. There were clouds of smoke billowing from the doorway, and several of the men began coughing. Colonel Hall tried waving away the smoke with his hands, to little avail, and they all stepped back to let the smoke dissipate.

"What's going on in there?" called one of the men in the back. Although he was shouting, the ears of the other men were ringing too loudly to hear. They each craned their necks to look inside.

The Colonel grabbed a file folder and began waving it in the air, in an attempt to disperse the smoke. Two other officers followed his lead, crowding into the doorway as they waved the manila folders. They began coughing immediately, but none of them wanted to be the first to quit.

Suddenly, one of the Suits ran up to the doorway carrying a fire extinguisher. He held it up to show Colonel Hall and said a few words that the Colonel couldn't hear, and the Colonel nodded his approval. He stepped back to let the man inside, and the Suit proceeded to unload the contents of the canister on a few fingers of fire that were scattered throughout the inside of the room. Coughing, he was forced to step carefully across the floor, which was littered with debris from the explosion. The man looked around and then, apparently satisfied, walked over to Colonel Hall.

"The area has been secured, Colonel," he said loudly as he placed the now-empty fire extinguisher at his feet. Even though he was no more than three feet away, the Colonel could barely hear the man, whose voice sounded muffled and distant.

"Thank you," said the Colonel. Unaware of the rank or position of the man in the suit, he didn't know if he should be authoritative or deferential, and tried to respond in as neutral a manner as possible.

Colonel Hall looked inside. Much of the smoke had indeed been scattered. Although there were no windows or other doors, there was an exhaust vent just inside the room, and it apparently drew out most of the fumes. At any rate, it was clear enough to see inside.

The Colonel tried to steel himself for the awful blood and carnage that was inevitable in the event of such an explosion as this. In his professional capacity, he had experienced a number of gruesome sights, and this day vowed to himself that he would not vomit at the mangled corpses of the three men he had seen enter the room. But the more he surveyed the scene of the blast, the more shocking was his growing realization. There was no blood. He saw no mangled limbs, no bits of flesh, bone, or muscle anywhere. He squinted, then rubbed his eyes in disbelief. It was impossible. Nothing remained in the room but the limp form of Crawford, slumped over in the far corner. A series of coughs told the Colonel that he was still alive.

"What just happened?" he wheezed.

The Colonel wondered the same thing. While he was chatting up a couple of presidential advisors, from the corner of his eye he had seen the Corporal enter the room with General Byrd and Mr. Crawford; they were supposed to brief Spumoni on the operation of the Time Hopper, then shuttle him through the press and a meet-and-greet involving a bunch of congressional wives. Bunch of crap, he thought to himself. At least this operation was back where it belonged—with the military.

But the men were obviously gone. With no windows or doors in the room, and no other way out, what the hell could have happened?

The Colonel heaved a deep sigh, and turned to one of the Suits. In the face of the impossible, he had no choice but to do the unthinkable.

"Call a medic. And get Hodges over here," he said quietly, "and hurry."

1768

When the Old Man stepped into the conference room, every eye was on him. He was always early for every meeting, and the others were shocked to see him scurry to his seat nearly ten minutes late. DaVinci knew it was to be a decisive meeting in the East Indian campaign, but unbeknownst to most of the participants, Lord North had a more ambitious agenda.

North stood at one end of the conference table, and another unfamiliar man stood beside him. Behind them were maps of North America and Australia, with a smaller map of China jutting out from behind Australia. Curious, thought DaVinci, for a meeting on India. He did note that the place at the table usually occupied by Benjamin Franklin was empty, and took that as a sign that his plan may not have been completely unsuccessful.

Then, the Old Man took a closer look at the unfamiliar person next to Lord North, and surmised that it must be the new Minister. None of the members of His Majesty's Inner Circle had met the Minister of Peace except for Lord North, and little was known about him. As the King became more delusional and paranoid, he started keeping his advisors separated as much as possible in order to discourage plotting against him.

The mysterious new Minister was believed to be from the Colonies, and there were rumors that some of the weaponry he had developed rivaled even that of the great DaVinci. He had apparently arrived a few months ago and was able to find favor with His Majesty and Lord North, much as he himself had done. He has his nerve, sniffed DaVinci. He had never met him—in fact, had never even seen him. He did know that the man's title had been created expressly for him, though his mission had little to do with peace.

Around the table, the various nobility and other favored advisors were sitting up in rapt attention, their eyes glued to the two men at the end of the table. Normally, a rare late arrival at a meeting of this sort was usually singled out for a few cutting remarks, but the rest of the King's Council seemed unnaturally quiet. Was it respect or fear? DaVinci didn't know, but thought it best to keep quiet until he could get a better sense of the mood in the room.

"Ah, Signor, very sorry but I'm afraid we had to begin without you," said North, apologizing with no trace of sincerity in his voice.

"Sorry, Your Excellency, but I was unavoidably detained," said DaVinci, bowing.

"If you don't mind, we'll carry on, and the introductions can wait until we're finished," said North.

DaVinci nodded and smiled. He pulled out a quill pen and a fresh piece of paper, then reached for an unclaimed bottle of ink in the center of the table.

"Now then, the Minister will show us the prototype of his automatic firing pistol," said North.

"Thank you," said the Minister, bowing slightly to Lord North.

He reached under the table and pulled out an object wrapped in canvas. As he spoke, he slowly unwrapped it, and every eye in the room was on him.

"The new 'miracle weapon,' as His Excellency is kind enough to describe it, has now been put into production not far from here," said the Minister. "The foundry is producing metal of a high enough quality for the triggering mechanism, and the finished models are being assembled in sufficient quantities to safeguard our troops."

He pulled the automatic pistol free of the canvas and held it up over his head with both hands. It was far and away more sophisticated than any of them would have thought possible. The men sitting around the table nodded their approval, even though none of them knew precisely what it was they were approving.

"This is not just any gun," interrupted Lord North.

"Correct, your Excellency," said the Minister. "This new advancement can fire 120 rounds per minute."

The men around the table stopped trying to look sophisticated for a moment and gasped at this impossibility.

"Actually, the biggest problem we're having at the moment is manufacturing sufficient ammunition," said the Minister. "This latest advance in weaponry will leave all other developments far behind."

He looked and appeared to pay attention to DaVinci for the first time.

"Even the most recent technology. Sorry, signor, I hope you don't mind," he said to the Old Man.

DaVinci smiled and waved his hand benignly. He had originally planned to use this meeting as an opportunity to discredit Franklin, but it appeared that a change of strategy would be necessary.

"If it's better for His Majesty, then I am happy," he replied, though he was inwardly furious at being upstaged. For years, he had been afraid of Franklin showing him up, and now? Now this American upstart is stealing his thunder with some fancy new superfast gun! He might just have to see about that.

"A company of His Majesty's finest, armed with these, will allow us to protect the Empire with an unsurpassed efficiency," said North

He turned to the maps hanging behind him.

"These are our trouble spots, the places that seem to be capable of challenging us," he explained, pointing to each as he described them.

"We all know about our problems in Canada and the American Colonies. There's Spain in the south and the French in Canada. Then, there are the savages on the frontier, preventing us from expanding to the west. But the biggest problem we've got is this insurrection that's been brewing for a while. Don't want to pay their taxes. They want a representative from the Colonies to sit with us. Can you believe such idiocy?

They're already being represented—by us!" The aristocrat laughed at this apparent ignorance, and the others around the table joined in.

He's sounding more arrogant than usual today, DaVinci thought to himself. He would not have made such an extreme statement if Franklin were still sitting at the table with the others. No matter how much Franklin bothered him, he could stand up for himself like no one else.

"We need to end talk of a Revolution, and the sooner the better," North continued. "Once that is finished, we may proceed to the equally important matters of ridding North America—and eventually both the American continents—of the Spanish and the French. Oh, and of course, we may find it necessary to exterminate the natives to ensure the safety of His Majesty's subjects in the New World."

DaVinci found himself growing very uncomfortable. He found words like "exterminate" extremely disconcerting. For the Old Man, the most unsettling aspect of it all was that he knew they could do what they were threatening. Even without this new rapid-firing gun, his own inventions—combined with Franklin's electrical discoveries—were enough to ensure their complete, bloody victory.

"We will use our land-based weaponry to further subdue the natives in India and the Far East," said North. "Using Bombay and Calcutta as our bases of operation in that region, we will expand our campaign in Hong Kong and throughout China."

Lord North pointed to the maps behind him as he spoke.

"With Hong Kong as our base, we will branch out across the countryside, along the Yangtze and capture Peking. It's all part of our battle to keep China British."

This is worse than I feared, thought DaVinci. They're actually planning to dominate the known world. And they're using my inventions to do it! He decided to test the waters and raised his hand tentatively.

"Are we expecting much resistance in those areas, your Excellency?" he asked. "And if there is, how well-equipped are we to deal with it?"

"Not to worry, signor," said North. "We will be giving your inventions an opportunity to be seen and used at every opportunity."

DaVinci smiled. Closer observers would have noted a rather sickly smile, if any of them had bothered to pay him much attention, but the rest of them were focused on the opportunities that war would present—especially the potential for such a one-sided war.

"In combination with our new firearms," North continued, "we will be able to dispatch any resistance that might be foolish enough to present itself in no time at all."

The others at the table all smiled at this, so DaVinci joined in. It didn't seem like a good idea to express his true feelings at this juncture.

Although DaVinci had experienced a few moments of uncertainty since first arriving in the future, until now he had not seriously questioned the King or his government. He had been content to provide the Crown with a few of his sketches and designs, in exchange for a mostly cushy existence as a court favorite. He had kept his nose out of politics, concentrating on inventions and the occasional painting of an influential aristocrat. Although he knew some of his projects were being applied toward more malevolent ends, he preferred not to think about it.

The King and his Court had always been somewhat contemptuous of the Colonists, and the farther flung the Colonies, the greater the disdain. Except for a few military and political appointees, they tended to be held in the same esteem as actors and prostitutes. This was typical of the aristocrats he had been familiar with, and so didn't bother the Old Man; in fact, he would have been suspicious if that had not been the case.

But now, something had changed. The arrogance, the casual disregard for innocent citizenry, the sense of entitlement that these aristocratic and military buffoons seemed to feel was vaguely rubbing him the wrong way. Their sudden shift in attitude startled him.

He'd seen greed and avarice in rulers before, but there was something in this calculated, premeditated destruction that just seemed wrong. With their new, ultra-sophisticated weapons of war, the revolutionaries and the natives wouldn't stand a chance. It would be cold-blooded murder, and it chilled him. Once they'd gotten a taste of victory, there was no telling how far they might be willing to go. They seemed awfully taken with the whole "British Empire" concept.

The Old Man decided to sit and keep his mouth shut, at least for now. He listened as Lord North and his new Minister of Peace charted what amounted to a course for world domination. They described how they would utilize DaVinci's discoveries and the new rapid-firing gun "to defend themselves against any violent resistance by the natives."

"And now, we have scheduled a presentation from Signor DaVinci to allow him to present his newest discoveries, which are also incorporating his latest electrical research," said Lord North.

God, here it was, the Old Man thought to himself. What was he to do? Could he stall them? Bluff? If they asked him any questions, he was stuck. Resigned to his fate, he feigned a cough as if to clear his throat, pushed his chair back and slowly rose to his feet.

"Oh, but I'm sorry, Signor," said North with a wave of his hand. "I know what we asked you to discuss, but I'm afraid we will not have enough time to review the specifics of your latest discoveries."

DaVinci could not believe his ears.

"Excuse me?" he asked.

"We'll have to postpone your discussion, I'm afraid," said North. "I apologize for not giving you more notice, but my manservant could not locate you earlier today. I'm very sorry."

DaVinci could not believe his luck.

"Of course, it is disappointing, but I understand," said the Old Man, nodding with just the right amount of disappointment in his voice.

"The British Empire stands on the brink of a new era of might and majesty, gentlemen," began North. "That greatness begins here. It starts with us, each of us in this room today. We are responsible for defending that greatness."

Oh, oh, thought DaVinci, here it comes.

"We have a duty to His Majesty and to God Almighty!" continued North. "We must bring civilization to the far corners of the globe! We have to defend our way of life, advance other countries to our standard—the British way of life. And God help any who stand in our way!"

There were cries of "Hear! Hear!" from various members of the council and moderate knocking on the table. This crowd was getting into the spirit of things, observed the Old Man.

"We Loyal Subjects have an obligation to do everything possible to convert the heathens, the foreign devils," he ranted. "And remember, there are those who will stop at nothing to destroy us. But thankfully, Our Lord has sent us two weapons to ensure our complete and utter triumph!"

He doesn't mean...? DaVinci thought to himself.

"And of course, I refer to our American friend and our Italian friend, who are with us today!" said North with another flourish.

Just what I needed, DaVinci thought to himself. *Another friend...*

Chapter Twenty

1848

"Are we getting a reading?" asked Sam.

"It's not moving," said Stan, who was sitting in the driver's seat.

Sam was under the Time Carriage, laying on his back and reaching into the instrument panel.

"It must be," said Jack. He was holding the schematics in his hands, carefully studying the wiring under the console. The three men were making what they hoped would be the final adjustments to the NLE, a curious hybrid that was part 19th Century carriage and part 21st Century Time Hopper.

Maggie pored over another copy of the plans, gradually deciphering futuristic symbols with a keen understanding that would shock most men of her era. She squinted at one diagram, placed it back on the workbench, and then got down on her hands and knees next to Sam. She looked carefully up at the instrument panel and noted his attempts to connect the wires.

"What's the matter, Maggie?" snapped Sam with a slightly sharp tone in his voice. He immediately regretted it, and realized he was taking out his frustrations on her.

"You've got it backward," she pointed out quietly.

"What are you talking about?" asked Sam, genuinely puzzled.

"The wires," she answered. "You've got them the other way around. The blue one is connected to the negative on that end, so it's got to be connected to the pole on the right under there."

She pointed as she spoke. Sam was so surprised to hear a woman talk about wiring that he failed to hear what she was trying to tell him.

"Uh, look, Maggie, maybe you'd best leave this to me and the others," said Sam, trying not to sound too patronizing.

"You might want to listen to her, Sam," said Jack. "She's a sharp one, believe me."

"Oh, yes, I'm sure she is," said Sam. "But I know how this is supposed to go together—"

Sam turned to look toward Jack, but found Maggie holding the schematics a few inches from his nose.

"Like I was sayin'—if you trace this wire here, where is it connected?" she told him slowly but firmly.

Sam was slightly startled to be so directly challenged, but after a moment studying the drawing, was more distressed to discover that she was right.

"Where'd you learn about electricity?" he asked.

"Just because I'm a woman doesn't mean I'm completely stupid," she glared at him. "Anyone with half a brain could figure out these plans."

"Sorry," he said quietly.

Jack watched her, mightily impressed. It seemed like the women of his time may be just as assertive and intelligent as Maggie, but none of them had her style or charm. For a woman of the mid-18th century, she stood alone. Despite the current disruption in the timeline, the other women of that era he had encountered seemed to be bland, deferential, and completely uninteresting. Whatever the differences in this world, the women's liberation movement had stayed far away.

Except for Maggie. She seemed little affected by the repressive social conventions of her era, and in fact, would be right at home in the 21st Century. But Jack knew better than anyone how impossible that would be. No, he would just have to make the most of his remaining time with her, until the present reality was terminated.

Jack had started to detach the wires at one end when Maggie heaved an exasperated sigh.

"Not that way!" she said. "Don't unhook them all. You don't—oh, never mind, just slide over."

Maggie got down on the ground and looked up at Sam's work. She then reconnected all but two of the wires that Sam had taken off.

"All you need to do is reverse these two wires," she told him, holding them out to Sam for a moment in case he decided to inspect them. Before he could react, she pulled them away and put them back under the console. She connected them to the proper poles, then quickly twisted them tight with a couple flicks of her wrist.

"You must have gone to school, Maggie," said Sam, intimidated and a little awestruck. Sarah had always wanted to study as well, but it was just too difficult, even for a person of Sam's station.

"Oh, I've done a little reading," she said. "Mostly on my own. My father always wanted a boy, and I think he was a little disappointed when I came along. But he tried to make up for it by giving me the best education he could. He taught me how valuable learning could be, and I've tried to make him proud."

"She's smart as a whip, Sam," said Jack. "In the past few days, I've learned it's generally best to just stand back and let her do what she does best. Usually, that's everything."

Maggie twisted her head out from beneath the NLE and called to Stan, who was bored by the whole exchange.

"Try it now," she said.

Stan watched, and to his surprise, the numbers on the gauge began rising.

"It works," he said to himself. The others heard him, however, and responded enthusiastically.

"Hoorah!" cheered Sam. He and Maggie both got up from the ground and dusted themselves off, broad smiles on their faces.

"Great job! That did it, Maggie!" said Jack.

"I know," said Maggie quietly.

"Now start it up," Jack said to Stan.

His partner hit the remaining buttons in the ignition sequence, and the engine fired up. The sound of its chugging was accompanied by a whole new round of cheering and backslapping. He let it run for a moment, then switched it off.

"Now what do we do?" asked Stan.

The others quieted at this thought. The moment that each of them, in their own way, never thought would arrive was now sitting in front of them. Now that they had the capability of making their immediate dreams come true, it was time to reassess those dreams.

"Uh—let's examine our options," said Jack. He always knew he would have to say goodbye to Maggie, but now that the moment was in sight, he was much less inclined to do so.

"I suppose now you can carry on..." said the unsmiling Maggie. "That's great." She had been so caught up in the excitement that she had likewise given little thought to the reality of their leaving.

"Yes, yes," said Sam. He was thrilled at the idea of traveling through time, but not at all happy at the idea of sharing his—their—discovery with Bonomi and giving him a ride through the Timestream. Still, when Bonomi had given him money, Sam had given him his word, and would have no choice. "I suppose I'd better summon Mr. Bonomi. We will undoubtedly need to depart soon."

"Undoubtedly, yes. Undoubtedly," said Stan. He was getting an uneasy feeling about the whole matter.

"I'd better tell Sarah, too," said Sam, fumbling with a few tools. After a few moments' silence, he added "You do know how to pilot it, of course?"

"Of course," said Stan.

There was another silence. Then, an agitated Jack burst out with a sudden thought.

"Mind you, there have been a few modifications to it all," he said. "I mean, I'm not 100-percent sure we could do it."

"What do you mean?" asked Stan. "Sam will be with us for the first trip."

"Oh, I know, I know," said Jack. "But I was just thinking that it would be even safer if we had somebody else riding along, somebody who knows all about it and could sort of integrate all of our designs and thoughts—"

"I'm going with you," said Maggie firmly.

"You?" asked Stan, the only one who hadn't seen it coming.

"Of course," she said. "I know it almost as well as you do, and I can even spot a few things that you can't."

"Well, I don't know..." said Sam.

"Maggie, that would be—I mean, are you sure?" asked a delighted Jack.

"Somebody has to look out for you," she said firmly.

"Come on, Sam, she could be a big help!" Jack pleaded.

"There is plenty of room," said Sam quietly, looking at the carriage. "With the four of us and Mr. Bonomi—"

"What?" Stan challenged him sharply.

"He has to go," said Sam. "He's part of our deal. Remember?"

"But—but—" protested Stan.

"He's got a point," Jack told his partner, then turned to Sam. "All right. He's in, but remember, we've got to fix the Time Stream. We can't do anything else to screw it up. And this is it. One trip, and one trip only."

"Yes, yes," said Sam, nodding impatiently.

"All right then, let's synchronize our watches," said Jack.

The others looked at him blankly.

"I'll tell you what, let's all just meet back here in an hour. Be ready for your first time hop."

"What should we bring with us? Is there anything we should do?" asked Sam.

"Yes," Jack said. "Don't bring any candy bars."

"That's going to be the least of your problems," said a voice from the doorway. It was American, and Jack swore it sounded familiar.

"Get away from that contraption, all of you!" ordered another voice, this one clearly British and crisp with menace. "I'm afraid this means you as well, Maggie!"

The four of them turned toward the entrance. James Burton stood with his gun leveled at the group. His Specserv uniform was neatly pressed and all the more ominous because of it. He looked deadly serious. Maggie started to speak, then thought the better of it.

"You're under arrest, all of you, and His Majesty is confiscating your machine here," said the American.

"Where is the other one? Bonomi? He's the only one missing," said Burton.

"He won't get far," said the American. "We'll pick him up after we deliver the prisoners—and their machine—to the Tower."

The American standing next to Burton was also holding what Jack recognized as some sort of automatic weapon. Jack looked at his face more closely. This American wore a British uniform similar to Burton's, but Jack could swear he recognized him. He just couldn't place him. The man seemed very familiar, yet very different.

"Call the rest of your men," the American said to Burton. "We can't let anything go wrong now!"

Then it struck him. Jack looked past the grey hair, beyond the wrinkles and receding hairline, into the eyes of the man before him.

The man he knew in another time as Corporal Frank Spumoni.

1768

"Dr. Franklin! Dr. Franklin!"

The Old Man called into the room, but there was no answer.

He tried the door handle. It was loose, but appeared to hold fast. He stepped back and threw his weight into it, and was surprised when it flew open in front of him.

He peered in, and looked at the American's living quarters. It had been ransacked. His desk drawers had been pulled out and dumped onto the carpet. Furniture was upside down, papers were strewn everywhere. The whole place was a dreadful mess.

"Dr. Franklin!" he called inside. "Are you in? Is there anyone there?"

There was a noise coming from the back.

"Who's there?" called DaVinci.

Franklin's manservant—wasn't his name "Eric?"—stuck his head out from an adjoining door. When he caught sight of DaVinci, he looked visibly relieved.

"Oh, Signor DaVinci!" he cried. "Thank heavens it's you!"

"Wha—?" gasped a startled DaVinci. The servant looked white as a sheet and trembled before him. "What happened?"

"It was terrible!" he trembled. "The soldiers came and when I didn't open the door fast enough, they pushed it in!"

The Old Man looked more closely, and saw that the doorframe around the handle had indeed been splintered. No wonder he had been able to push it in so easily.

"Calm yourself now," said DaVinci, taking the man's arm and placing his still-trembling form on the couch. "Do you want something to drink?"

The man shook his head no.

"Now then, tell me what happened here," he said, still puzzled but trying to maintain his own composure. "First of all, where is Dr. Franklin?"

"I—I don't know, sir," stammered Eric. "He hasn't been home all day. I—I thought he was going to meet with you this morning."

"Yes, of course," said DaVinci. "He did do that, but he didn't show up at the meeting with Lord North. What happened here?"

"There was a pounding at the door, but before I could open it, half a dozen of the King's soldiers burst right in, they did, just like they owned the place!" said Eric, slowly building up momentum as he spoke. "They demanded to know where

Dr. Franklin was. I told them I didn't know, I-I hadn't seen him since he left this morning."

"Calm down," said DaVinci.

"They wanted to know where he kept his papers, and I said I couldn't tell them. They got angry and pushed me away. They started looking all around. They were going through his drawers and cupboards, pulling things out and just throwing them to the floor, very casually! Just like they knew I'd have to pick them up."

"Is that how all this happened?"

He gestured to the debris strewn across the floor.

"That's right. It's going to take a fortnight to clean this place! I don't know why they—"

"And so then what happened?"

Eric paused for a moment to get back on track.

"Well, they kept looking. They finally found the desk in his study and began going through it."

He walked to the back of the room, stepping carefully over the rubble, and looked through the doorway.

"There it is."

DaVinci walked to his side and Eric pointed inside the room. The Old Man peered inside and saw what was left of his study.

The desk drawers had been emptied, and the contents dumped on the floor. The books had been pulled off the shelves and scattered around the room as well.

"They looked through it all, but didn't take anything," said Eric. "Apparently, they didn't find what they were looking for."

"Do you know what were they trying to find?"

"I believe they were looking for papers of some sort."

Uh oh, thought DaVinci to himself. *No doubt they were after the incriminating papers that I planted on him this morning.*

"They couldn't find them in here, so they got angry," continued Eric. "They came back out and cut the cushions open on the chairs and sofas, and reached inside. Just like they thought there was something hiding inside."

He walked back out and the Old Man followed quickly behind. Eric pointed to the chairs and sofas. Most of the stuffing had been pulled out and tossed around the room.

"Look at that. You'd think they could have been a little more neat about it, don't you?

"Uh..."

"You know who has to clean all of that up, don't you?"

"I'm sorry."

"When I started picking it up, they hit me! Can you believe that? A loyal subject like myself?"

"I hope you weren't hurt."

"I bruise very easily!"

"Would you like some help picking things up? I could send my manservant—"

"No, thank you. That's really not the point."

Clearly he is losing control, thought the Old Man.

"Perhaps I'd better go. I—I can see if Dr. Franklin has been seen anywhere else—" said DaVinci, taking a step toward the door.

"I work my fingers to the bone to keep this place clean, and then this happens!" said Eric, palms raised toward the ceiling as he looked around. He was becoming oblivious to the Old Man, who took advantage of the fact to start backing more quickly toward the exit.

"No one appreciates it anyway!" Eric continued. "I polish every stick of wood in here until it shines—you can see yourself in it—"

"Good luck to you, my friend!" said the Old Man. He had to find out if he had gotten the American arrested or worse. It was looking like the chubby little doctor was his only chance to prevent the British domination of the entire world—and he was the only one who could save him.

DaVinci reached the door, gave a small wave of his hand and dashed off, heading down the hallway.

"Fine, fine," muttered Eric. "Don't bother to help..."

Chapter Twenty-One

1848

"It's you!" gasped Stan. "But you got old!"

"Yes, and it's your fault!" accused Corporal Spumoni. "That's what happens when you get launched hundreds of years back into time looking for a couple of morons!"

"You mean us?" asked Stan.

"And then the military either can't or won't come after you. And you start to get older and older until you resign yourself to the fact that you're going to die hundreds of years before you were born!" ranted the Corporal. "So what if you can't fix their stupid Chronological Anomaly? Who cares what happens to 'em? They're hundreds of years in the future. Screw 'em!"

"But—but we've got the Time Machine fixed and ready to go! Just put down the gun and you can go back home!" urged Jack.

Burton looked alarmed. He turned toward Corporal Spumoni, a concerned look in his eye.

"Don't listen to them," warned Burton.

"James, how could you? How can you be this way?" said Maggie, batting her eyes and with a hurt expression on her face.

"It won't work, Maggie," he said coldly.

"You wouldn't shoot me," Maggie said to him. Though he still kept it lowered, Burton turned the barrel in her direction.

"Don't try me, Maggie," he said with an iciness in his voice that frightened her. "I have my orders. It would pain me to carry them out, but I would indeed."

Maybe he would at that, thought Maggie. She knew he wouldn't hesitate to shoot Jack, Stan and Sam.

Burton shot an accusing look at the Corporal, who shook his head.

"Don't worry," Spumoni told Burton. "I got a nice soft job and a pretty easy life right here. I'm not going to do anything to screw it up."

"Hey, you're not a Corporal anymore!" Stan blurted out, noticing his new uniform, complete with epaulets and braiding, for the first time. Spumoni, suddenly taking notice of Stan, turned slowly toward him, but before either of them could speak, Sam broke the silence.

"I don't understand," said Sam, completely confused by the events of the past sixty seconds. "If you're from the future, too, then where's your Time Machine?"

"Gone," said Corporal Spumoni. "After I accidentally hit the self-destruct button, I jumped off and landed back here. God knows where it blew up, but it took General Byrd with it."

Jack clutched at his chest.

"G-general Byrd?" he sputtered. "The General Byrd?"

"He got caught up in things," shrugged the Corporal. "The NLE-X dragged him along. Last I saw of him, he was heading toward the eighteenth century, if he survived."

"Holy shit!" exclaimed Stan. "We've got to pick him up too? We'll never get the Timeline fixed!"

"I wouldn't worry too much about the General or the Time Hopper," said the Corporal. "He wouldn't jump off, so he was blown to bits when the whole thing self-destructed."

"This is just getting worse and worse..." said Jack to himself quietly. "So you're not going to come with us?"

"On the contrary," said Burton, raising his weapon. "You are coming with us."

"No, Jack, no!" cried Maggie. She batted her eyes at Burton, feigning a combination of disbelief, innocence and good old-fashioned sex appeal, with enough of the latter to nearly spark a protest from Jack. Burton wanted to believe her but couldn't quite buy into it. With a pained expression, she took a step toward him. When Burton turned to look at her, he dropped his guard for just a moment. It was enough for Stan to drop a piece of firewood on his head.

When Jack saw what was happening, he wasted no time. As Corporal Spumoni shifted his eyes to watch what was happening to his partner, Jack kicked the weapon up and out of his hand. It spun slowly into the air as all of them but Burton watched, as though it had caught them by surprise.

"Get it!" Jack called to Stan, who was closest to Corporal Spumoni.

Stan and the Corporal recovered simultaneously, and both jumped for the weapon as though it were a loose basketball. Sam and Jack followed, bumping into them and knocking them down. Stan's fingertips brushed against the barrel, knocking it away, and the four men all fell to the ground in a tangle of limbs. Meanwhile, the handgun continued its own trajectory. When it struck the ground, the impact caused it to start spitting bullets, its rapid-firing barrel a blaze of smoke and flame.

The men, who had climbed free of each other, immediately dove to the floor, attempting to dodge the torrent of shots. Although it seemed to be spraying the entire room, less than a dozen rounds had discharged in less than a second, and none of them found a human target.

In fact, only one bullet did any damage at all. It struck the top of the Time Carriage, and before it passed through and lodged in the wooden ceiling, it had severed a pair of wires.

1768

Lord North pulled the door open to find DaVinci knocking furiously.

"What's this all about, Signor?" he asked.

The Old Man burst inside and began pacing.

"Thank you, your Excellency," he said. "In all honesty, I am concerned about the situation involving Dr. Franklin."

Lord North smiled and nodded.

"Ah, of course, Signor," he said. "I must apologize for not informing you of the latest developments with the good doctor, for which we are all in your debt, sir."

DaVinci gulped and said "Very good of you."

"I understand you informed the King's Guard that you were successful in your attempt to—" said North, who shifted uncomfortably. "That after Dr. Franklin was finished visiting with you this morning, some very important documents of yours were later found to be missing."

"Yes, sir."

"And these were believed to be rather—sensitive documents."

"That's right sir."

"Well, after you reported to us, we immediately began the search for the American," said North. "And you'll be happy to learn that we expect to apprehend him very soon."

"Very soon?"

"That's correct, very soon. And it's all thanks to you."

"So you haven't caught him yet?"

"No, but we expect to. Very soon," said North, smiling.

Then it may not be too late, DaVinci thought to himself. *Now if I were Franklin, where would I go to hide?*

1848

In the end, they'd had to run, of course.

Corporal Spumoni had somehow managed to end up with the gun, despite the desperate grasping of the others. He gripped it tightly, and started to swing it around toward the others, his finger tensed upon the trigger. It was clear he was ready to aim and fire.

The other men took a step back. But Maggie grasped the gravity of their situation as well. She immediately flung the only object she was holding toward Corporal Spumoni's gun hand.

Amazing no one more so than herself, the object struck the Corporal's gun and dislodged it from his hand.

Unfortunately, the only object she was holding turned out to be the gun she had plucked from Burton's unconscious hand. Once again, they were defenseless, and the only two guns were inches away from the Corporal's hands. Stan had watched it all transpire and shouted his immediate assessment.

"Run!" he cried.

No one argued. Sam and Stan scrambled to the door, while Jack made sure that Maggie got out safely before him. Corporal Spumoni fumbled for the guns.

"Hurry!" urged Jack. As Maggie clambered out the door, Jack followed on her heels, less than a second before the Corporal began shooting. The bullets passed through the boards next to the door like a warm knife cutting into butter. The first spray of lead narrowly missed Jack. The Corporal would never have taken so long to get a shot off when he was in his prime, thought Jack to himself. In fact, his advanced age might be their only hope of outrunning him.

In the lead, Sam and Stan zigged to the right and zagged left, with Maggie and Jack right behind. The Corporal, who was foolishly trying to run while carrying two automatic pistols, was starting to lose ground. He squeezed off several more rounds, but missed Maggie and Jack by a wider margin, just before they turned a corner.

"Hurry up!" Maggie cried.

"We—we better split up!" wheezed Stan. "M-meet us—"

"Meet us at Bonomi's house in an hour!" Sam gasped. "Just—just a block south of here, the big grey place."

"Yeah!" said Jack, then turned his head slightly to address Maggie, who was alongside him. "Do—do you know—"

"Don't worry," she answered.

As the four of them reached another intersection, Sam stuck out his hand and pointed to the right. He veered down the road to the right and Stan followed. Jack and Maggie turned sharply down the road to the left.

A block behind them, the former Corporal raced as quickly as his now-middle-aged legs could carry him, while he quietly cursed to himself. He watched as they split up, wondering who he should follow. Though he still carried both guns in his hands, he was too far away to attempt a shot. He wasn't unconcerned about the half-dozen innocent passersby along the way, but he was enough of a realist to know he could never hit any of them, particularly with the way his hands were shaking. Still, he wasn't ready to give up. If he couldn't stop them, he could at least let them know they'd been in a chase.

As he approached the intersection, he knew he had to make a decision. In a split-second, the male chauvinist area of his brain told him he might have a better chance of catching the woman, and he found himself veering to the left.

Though they were building a commanding lead, both Jack and Maggie sensed the Corporal behind them as he turned the corner to continue his pursuit. Jack found himself struggling to keep pace with Maggie, who had kicked off her shoes to run along the cobblestones. There were more pedestrians on the sidewalk and vehicles on this street, to say nothing of the occasional flying machine passing overhead. He would have a harder time shooting at them now.

"I know where we are," Maggie said in a lowered voice. "Keep close to me. We're going to make a few sharp turns."

No sooner were the words out of her mouth than she cut across him and turned left, heading down a narrow alley at top speed. Jack nearly stumbled, but followed as best he could. Another hundred feet, Maggie turned left again. This time Jack kept up, and they stepped onto a wider thoroughfare dotted with shops and increasing numbers of people.

"Not much further," encouraged Maggie.

Jack, who felt his lungs burning, knew he couldn't last much longer.

Maggie scanned the street as she ran, looking at the shop windows. Suddenly her face lit up in recognition.

"I know where we are," she said, panting.

"What?" gasped Jack. The kind, benevolent part of him was happy that Stan and Sam were apparently going to get away, but the part of himself that he was in touch with on a more regular basis cursed his luck, along with those two rotten bastards skittering away like rats into an alleyway.

"This way," said Maggie, making a small gesture to the left. They rounded the corner and found themselves in an open square that was surrounded by more shops and dozens, perhaps hundreds, of people. Here they would have no choice but to slow down to make their way through the throngs.

"Maybe we can lose ourselves in the crowd," said Jack, though secretly, he was relieved to be able to slow down.

"No!" snapped Maggie, who was hustling as quickly as possible. "Follow me!"

"Where?" asked Jack, hoping he didn't sound too whiny. He knew from personal experience that there were few traits less attractive to females.

At least they had to keep a slower pace, thought Jack. If they had kept up their previous speed much longer, he was certain he'd have a grabber, right there in the 19th Century.

"Right up there!" Maggie indicated, nodding her head in the direction of a shop near the end of the block. "That's where I got my flying machine!"

Rounding the corner a half block behind them was the Corporal. He plunged into a large group of women chatting nearby. He startled them with his sudden appearance and his guns, but their agitation inadvertently made it even more difficult for him to get by.

Maggie and Jack wove through the crowd until they reached the front door of the shop, Maggie grabbed him by the sleeve and pulled him along as she entered. But just before he stepped inside, Jack spotted Corporal Spumoni talking with half a dozen uniformed Specserv agents. They were looking toward him as the Corporal pointed in his direction. But before he could react, he was inside the shop, where Maggie finally loosened her grip on his sleeve.

The place was much larger than it looked from the street. There was an open atrium, and from the cathedral ceiling, half a dozen flying rigs were hanging. The second and third balconies surrounded the displays, and a couple of well-to-do customers were inspecting the machines.

One clerk on duty smiled in recognition as Maggie stepped up to him.

"Hello, I'd like to—" she began, but the salesman cut her off.

"Not to worry, it's all fixed!" he beamed. "It's on the top level. I can have someone bring it down for you if—"

Before he could finish, Maggie had brushed past him heading for the stairs, nodding to Jack to follow her.

"No need for that," she said, abrupt but smiling. "It works fine, then?"

"Oh, yes, good as new!" beamed the clerk. "Of course, you have to be careful with these things."

But Maggie showed no interest in talking with him and hurried up the steps, as Jack struggled to keep up. They finally arrived on the top level, in what was obviously a workshop area. Several sets of wings were strewn around the room in various stages of repair, while a few were off to the side, stacked neatly on a bench.

"Does it look okay, Miss Wells?" called the clerk from below.

She pushed a bench beneath a skylight and climbed up.

"We have to hide," she explained quietly. "Let's get on the roof."

Jack walked over to the window that overlooked the entrance, and his fears were realized. Half a dozen Specserv agents, led by Corporal Spumoni, were at the front door.

"Too late for that now," he warned her. "They're here."

"Fine—my friend here is going to need one, too," she called down to the clerk. "But don't tell anybody we're here. And I'd like it all billed to James Burton."

"He'll be happy to know you're thinking of him!" Corporal Spumoni's voice shot up at the two of them.

He turned to the group of Specserv agents gathered around him and barked "They're upstairs. They're trapped, so don't let them get away!"

The Corporal scurried to the stairway, with the other men at his heels, and began climbing up, two steps at a time.

"Is there something I can help you with?" the clerk called behind him.

Their boots pounded on the boards below as they hurried toward the top level. The Corporal was mounting the steps three at a time, and the other men hustled to keep up with him.

Finally, their leader reached the third floor, springing into the room anxiously. A quick scan found only various makes and models of flying machines, some of them brand new, others recently repaired. The Specserv agents behind him began a quick visual search of the room.

"They've got to be here!" snarled Corporal Spumoni. "Look! Keep looking! There's no way out."

While there may not have been any way out of the room, it was just as obvious that there was nobody else in the room at the moment. The men looked at each other, gave a slight shrug of the shoulders, and then did their best to look as though they were intently searching. They fanned out, peeking under impossibly small pieces of debris, while the Corporal fumed. He leaned against a small workbench in the center of the room. It was obvious they were no longer here. But where? He heard them just as he walked into the shop, didn't he?

And then he looked up.

Directly overhead was a shutter covering a large skylight. Could it be?

The sound of a board creaking in the roof was enough to convince him that he was right.

"That's enough!" he ordered. The men slowly stopped their searching, looked toward him and listened for his next set of commands. The Corporal put one finger to his lips to indicate silence, then pointed upward with the other hand.

The men followed his finger and looked up to see the skylight, and even the dimmest of them understood.

"We've got them trapped up on the roof," whispered the Corporal. "There's no way they can get down now, unless we bring them down. So let's go get them!"

And the six men began piling furniture beneath the skylight.

Chapter Twenty-Two

1848

Jack could hear their boots approaching from his vantage point on the roof, and he became increasingly nervous as they got nearer.

"They made it to the top!" he whispered fearfully. "I think they're coming up!"

"Get ready," Maggie responded, sliding her hands into the straps on her wings.

Jack had already been fitted with his flying machine. Maggie had helped strap the harness on him. For all intents and purposes, he was ready to take off. Unfortunately for her, Jack's intent was to remain on the roof for the purpose of staying alive.

"No!" said Jack, panicking. "I mean—why don't we wait until we know for sure that they're onto us."

"I already explained to you," she said, "that flying is safer than riding in a motorcar."

"Why don't we test that out? You fly, while I take a motorcar?" he joked nervously.

"Jack, you know how to use it," she said patiently. "You keep pedaling and lean your body in the direction you want to go. Stay close to me. But not too close or we'll crash."

"There's a comforting thought," he said. "Are you sure this damned thing is safe?"

Like Maggie, he was inside the harness underneath the framework. The bat-like wings spread out about eight feet and flapped when he pedaled. There were pedals near his feet, and two straps hung down within reach of his hands. In principle, it reminded him of an ultra-lite plane, except ultra-lites had motors.

Jack looked down and trembled. He was not encouraged. It was a much further drop to the ground than it looked when he was on the street. He had decided not to tell her about his extreme fear of heights, but worried he would soon give himself away.

"You need a running start," continued Maggie. "We're up fairly high, which should help, but when you leap from the roof, start pedaling as fast as you can."

"You mean I can't start pedaling until after I leap off?"

Maggie chuckled. "Oh, Jack, you're so funny! Of course not, you have to get a running start!"

Apparently, his terror had not yet begun to show.

"I've got an idea," he stalled. "Maybe you should go and I should stay here, to hold them off and make sure you get away—"

"Don't be silly, Jack," she said. "He's got two guns and he's a very good shot. But it's very sweet of you to be concerned."

Jack gave her a sickly smile. She had given him something else to worry about. If he stayed on the roof, he was dead as well. But at least he wouldn't be plunging to his death. The fear of falling weighed heavily on him.

"Get ready," said Maggie.

Carrying the framework of the flying machine she was encased in, Maggie carried it over to the edge of the roof.

"Jack! They're here!" hissed Maggie.

And sure enough, he could hear the skylight being smashed open. A shot rang out.

Yes, falling was worse than being shot, wasn't it? And if he stayed there, he might not even be shot, he reasoned to himself. Maybe he'd even be able to talk some sense into the Corporal.

"Let's kill 'em!" a familiar voice cried.

Unless, of course, living the past 30 years in the 19th Century had driven him insane, thought Jack. And of course, there was always the chance he could be shot and not die, but fall off the roof afterward. That would be an awful irony, getting shot and falling to his death afterward.

"Jack!" shrieked Maggie. "Come on!"

The first of the Specserve agents scrambled onto the roof.

"They're going to jump!" he called to the others inside. "We may need flying machines!"

As the second man clambered up, they both pulled their guns out of their harnesses.

"Now!" screamed Maggie.

She ran the last three paces to the edge of the roof and leaped into the air. For a split-second, it seemed as though she was going to plunge straight down. Then, the wind seemed to catch and lift her. While she was not gaining altitude, neither was she losing any. She began to pedal, and with bat-wings slowly flapping and a small propeller behind her turning, she sped up.

Jack stood with his heart in his mouth, too petrified to move.

While Corporal Spumoni climbed through the skylight onto the roof, the two Specserv agents raised their weapons and aimed.

"Jack!" screamed Maggie. "Come on, love!"

In the split-second that followed, he tried to comprehend what he had just heard. Did she really call him "Love?" And did she mean "Luv," like the British slang for the shopkeeper getting your fish 'n chips so he'd give you extra chips? Or did she mean "Love," as in—well—Love?

Fear of heights or not, he would have to find out.

With three long strides and without thinking any more, Jack lunged for the edge of the roof and leaped off. He was struck by the pleasant realization that he wasn't plunging to his death.

And then he looked forward to see a huge cathedral looming just ahead. He was heading straight for it at a pretty fair speed. Without looking, his trembling hands reached for the straps that would help him steer. The flying machine banked to the right, missing the steeple by less than a foot.

At that point, he noticed the ground was rapidly approaching. *This isn't good,* he thought to himself.

Suddenly, something came whizzing past his head, and Jack realized that in all the excitement, he nearly hadn't noticed the loud bang from behind. He felt strangely invigorated. *What was it Churchill had said? Or would be saying? There was nothing more exhilarating to be shot at without result.* He started to smile, when half a dozen other rounds came heading in his direction. One came within a few inches and another pierced a wing, leaving a tiny round hole. *It was going to be,* Jack realized, *what the pilots referred to as a "brown trouser flight."*

Jack hoped they couldn't hit a moving target. He started pedaling as quickly as possible, and began to level off. Just as Maggie had promised, the craft started skyward again. *Maybe this is not my day to die,* Jack thought for the first time in the last ten minutes.

About a hundred yards ahead, Maggie was riding the wind currents as gracefully as a bird. She turned her head, craning her neck as she looked for him.

"Maggie!" he called.

She twisted her head even further, and her face lit up.

"Jack!" she shouted. She stopped pedaling, gliding in order to slow down, and Jack began pedaling all the harder to get closer to her.

Jack finally started to relax. Their pursuers were getting farther and farther behind them. He soon found himself alongside of Maggie, about twenty feet away to her right.

"How are you doing?" she called over to him.

"I'm—I'm fine," he answered, surprised to find that he really meant it.

"It's fun, isn't it?" she asked. "The wind in your face? The empty sky in front of you? Free as a bird!"

"It is fun at that, isn't it?"

"Why don't we circle back and head over toward the Thames?" Maggie suggested.

"Good idea," Jack answered. He figured that way, if they plummeted to the ground, they'd end up hitting water. He wasn't a terribly strong swimmer, but knew his chances were better than if he hit the cobblestone pavement.

They soared in a wide arc, eventually heading back in the direction they had come from. As Jack spotted the rooftop that he had leaped from only a few minutes ago, he was starting to feel more in control.

"Is there somebody down there?" Maggie called to him, nodding in the direction of the rooftop.

"Of course not," Jack shouted. "There's nothing to be worried about. Those Specserv clowns are a mile away by now!"

He glanced back at the rooftop they had just flown over, and saw three of those Specserv clowns emerging from the skylight.

"What are they doing?" Jack said to himself. He didn't want to alarm Maggie, but decided to circle back once more for a quick look, just in case. He pulled the left strap down hard, and the flying machine made a sharp turn to the left.

On the rooftop, just in front of him, seven Specserv agents were now pulling flying machines out through the skylight, assembling and strapping them on. There were seven men with flying machines all together.

Suddenly, one of them looked up and pointed directly at Jack.

"That's him!" he shouted. "That's one of them!"

"After him!" barked Corporal Spumoni. "Don't let him— or the girl—get away!"

Jack hoped that didn't mean what he knew it did. As he began pedaling madly for his life, he began stealing glances backward.

Two by two, the flying machines were lifted from the roof by the wind currents. These were undoubtedly experienced fliers who knew how to make these machines sing.

At least Maggie is far off by now, he thought to himself. Then he raised his head and saw her heading toward him.

"Maggie!" he called frantically. "Go back!"

Jack gestured frantically and she smiled and waved back at him.

"Maggie! No!" he shouted. "They're coming after us!"

Maggie cocked her head to one side and turned her palms up to signal her non-comprehension. Jack could see the moment her eyes caught the squadron of agents taking to the air. She nearly stopped short—a most difficult feat in mid-air—and she somehow pivoted her machine 180-degrees and accelerated. She offered Jack some encouragement.

"Hurry up or they'll kill you!" she screamed.

That was a powerful incentive, he thought, but not as powerful as knowing that she cared. Or at least didn't want to see him killed. *As reasons to live go, I'll take what I can get.*

Jack gathered speed, and would have passed Maggie if she hadn't started pedaling by that point. The seven Specserv agents were a good fifty yards behind Jack and Maggie. It had become a sprint, rather than a marathon, but no one seemed to be gaining or losing. Jack didn't know about the others, but he was getting winded.

About thirty feet away, Maggie gave him a quick nod, then dropped out of the sky in what Jack recognized as a dive roll. She sped toward the ground at nearly a 90-degree angle, spinning as she dove. Maggie stole a glance back at him, a fierce, frantic look that seemed to order him to follow.

"Oh, no, Maggie," Jack muttered to himself, "I can't. Don't ask me. Anything but that."

Jack decided to take his chances in the air. Granted, the Specserv agents were nasty, but he had a reasonable lead built up, and he thought he could maintain it. And then he saw the guns.

All seven fliers were holding them as they pedaled furiously.

This may require a re-think, Jack decided.

They were not going to be able to aim, let alone fire their weapons if they were racing along so quickly, he reasoned. And then a series of shots rang out, whizzing a few inches past his head.

Jack began heading directly toward the ground below. Maggie was ahead of him, still spinning as she fell, reminding him of a World War I flying ace.

I got you into this, he thought as he watched her plunge toward the ground. *If anything happens to you, it'll all be my fault.*

And then, Maggie pulled out of her dive. She managed to level off her flying machine about twenty feet before crashing, parallel to the ground for a moment, and flying along a street between a long row of tall buildings on either side before she started climbing again.

But Jack had no time to admire her style. Two of the Specserv agents in their flying machines were on his tail. With the ground rushing up at him, he immediately flung his arms back and extended his body until the wings started to level off. Jack realized he was pulling up. But the street still loomed, now forty, now thirty feet below him. He stretched, bending as far back as he could extend. *Twenty feet, now ten, now—ten?* He was remaining at ten feet high. No, he was—climbing?

He was going to live.

And at that same moment, he heard two loud crashes, almost simultaneously. He stole a quick glance back, only to see the two lead Specserv fliers in a pile of rubble on the ground.

His guilt lasted until the next burst of gunfire in his direction. The rest of them had negotiated the turn with ease, which left them free to aim and fire their weapons at him.

Jack found himself flying about thirty feet above the streets. The tall buildings that lined the streets made him feel like he was soaring along through a canyon with hundred-foot walls. They were not skyscrapers by 21st Century standards, but such heights were virtually unthinkable for the mid-19th Century. He held steady at thirty feet, deciding he would be much more vulnerable if he flew to the top, and if he made it, the more experienced fliers would have the advantage.

Peering a couple of blocks ahead, he saw a pair of flapping wings. Maggie appeared to be trying to catch his attention and almost hovered while he drew closer. As he came within a block of her, she accelerated and tried to keep pace with him.

"What are you doing?" he shouted. "Don't wait for me!"

"Follow me!" she commanded.

"All right," he answered. "But no more diving!"

Maggie sped off, leaving him feeling like he was standing still. Then, she made a sharp left turn down an alley no more than twenty feet ahead. Jack narrowly followed, and heard the cloth of his right wing scrape against the building.

He somehow leveled off and regained his composure, then began pedaling anew.

Suddenly he heard a crunching sound from behind. He glanced back just in time to see one of the Specserv fliers flattened against the brick wall of the alleyway, with scattered pieces of his now-shattered flying machine falling to the ground below him. He remained plastered against the wall, apparently defying the laws of gravity, for what felt like several moments. Then, he slowly seemed to peel away and fall toward the ground, suggesting a real-life version of a Warner Brothers Roadrunner cartoon.

The other four were forced to slow down to avoid striking the wreckage of their colleague (and the colleague himself). One of them overshot the alley entirely, wasting several moments before backtracking into the narrow lane.

Jack was much more concerned with catching up to Maggie. She made another sharp left turn down another alleyway, an even sharper, more treacherous turn into an even narrower alley than the last.

Without stopping to think, he immediately gave a sharp pull on the strap in his left hand. He felt the left wing dip and the right wing rise high into the air, fifty, sixty, now at a seventy-degree angle. He took his feet off the pedals and held them out to his side in an unconscious attempt to keep his balance.

His wings were now nearing the far corner at a ninety-degree angle, but they weren't turning sharply enough. He was going to hit the wall, and if the collision didn't kill him, the fall surely would.

But as his legs flailed helplessly, thrown out by the centrifugal force, he felt one toe brush up against a brick. Without thinking, he tried to kick away as best he could, only to find his other foot coming in contact with the wall. Since he was not being crunched into the wall as much as he was dragged along its surface, he could almost run along the outside of the wall while thirty-feet up. And so he continued, skittering along, perpendicular to the wall, almost fun in a terrifying sort of way.

He pushed off one last time and aimed his wings out into the open space between the two rows of buildings. The air caught them and buoyed him up. He placed his feet on the pedals, and once again he was flying.

There was another sharp thud behind him, a sound that Jack was starting to associate with good news. Sure enough, another of the Specserv fliers had failed to negotiate the turn. Failed rather miserably, he noted upon glancing back. This particular pursuer had slammed rather soundly into the brick wall, demolishing one wing. He fell away from the wall but never stopped pedaling, and plummeted to the ground with the undamaged wing fluttering impotently.

That was the good news, Jack thought to himself. The bad news was that the other three were still racing after him. He looked straight ahead and his eyes grew wide in panic. It was like a scene from an early 20th century tenement neighborhood. Several clotheslines were strung from building to building, with varying amounts of laundry hanging from them. If the Corporal had deliberately designed an obstacle course, he could not have done a better job. It was too late to fly above or below the tangle of cords and wet clothes; he was somehow going to have to fly through and avoid them all.

Maggie had cleared the whole mess by the time Jack flew over the first line, dodging it by several feet. A dress and several pairs of trousers threatened to tangle in his wings, but he slipped between the next two lines.

His pursuers showed no signs of letting up. The two men closest to Jack soared into the jumbled mass of wires. One of them negotiated the obstacles skillfully, but the other got his right wing caught in a rope, his forward momentum nearly tearing it from the harness. He grabbed the clothesline just in time and hung on for dear life. The third man soared up above the whole expanse of ropes and clothing, though he was slowing down considerably. He reminded Jack of an elderly man trying to bicycle up a steep hill, and having considerable difficulty.

There was only the one Specserv flier left to worry about, Jack realized. Unfortunately, he was the man soaring effortlessly through the ropes, holding his gun in one hand as he flew.

There was still one final obstacle of ropes ahead, made all the worse by the wall of laundry. Jack soared straight into a large white bed sheet. His momentum knocked it free of the rope as it completely covered the front of his body. He tried peeling it off, but the winds in front of him kept it whipping right back, covering his face. Which may have been just as well, as Jack likely would have panicked when he saw that he was heading into the side of a building.

But the remaining Specserv flier kept coming, unholstering and aiming his gun. *He's too close to miss,* Jack thought to himself.

As Jack pulled the sheet free, the wind slammed it into the Specserv flier behind him. The sheet enveloped his arm just as his gun began firing, and the bullets went flying off into the distant sky. His face and upper body were covered, and his feet became tangled in the pedals and the cloth.

Panicking, the Specserv flier started pedaling faster, but by that point, the pedals were not connected to any of the drive mechanisms. Without the power to keep his flying machine in the air, he began to lose altitude. Quickly.

Jack made it through the ladies' undergarments that hung on the final set of clotheslines and glanced back once again, only to see the agent in the flying machine heading toward the ground below. Had he truly managed to out-maneuver seven trained fliers in his very first flight?

A short distance ahead, Maggie was flying as close as she dared, occasionally stealing a glance behind to make sure Jack was safe.

"Maggie!" he called to her. "We did it!"

She turned her head back toward him, smiling. She looked as though she was about to speak. Then suddenly, her mouth dropped open and she let out a scream.

Puzzled, he looked behind him. There was nothing following. He looked below, then scanned the skies in front of him. Nothing.

"Maggie, relax!" he shouted.

Maggie continued speeding away.

"Above!" she cried without turning around.

And at that moment, the words freshly out of her mouth, she took a sharp turn at the next street.

Jack craned his neck back, looking up this time. There, aiming his automatic straight down at him, was Corporal Spumoni.

Jack felt like a sitting duck as several rounds from the Corporal's automatic whizzed past.

He careened into the next street, glancing backward as the Corporal kept up his pursuit. His wings tilted at a 45-degree angle, presenting the Corporal with an irresistible target. He squeezed off several more rounds, tearing a large portion of Jack's left wing to shreds.

Jack felt the flying machine start to shimmy, and his balance was thrown off. There might be enough canvas on the wing to prevent a crash, but his flying abilities were seriously impaired.

And then he looked forward.

What he thought was a bustling, wide-open street had been turned into a cul-de-sac. A towering fifteen-story Victorian skyscraper lay dead ahead.

Maggie was trying to climb even higher to retreat from the Corporal's guns, but Jack would not have the time, space or maneuvering capability to escape in such a manner, even if he hadn't lost half of his left wing. He headed for the wall of the building straight ahead, with a maniacal time-traveling corporal aiming 21st Century guns at him.

If he slowed down or even tried to turn, he would certainly plummet to the ground—unless the Corporal blasted him apart first. With his torn wing, he couldn't fly upward. It appeared that all he could look forward to in the few moments remaining in his life was flying splat into the side of a building.

The cliché appeared to be true. Time seemed to freeze enough to allow him to think.

During the next moment, he realized that he was actually in control of his own fate. Guns? Falling? Splatting? It really was his decision. He felt a little better. He considered them all briefly, much as he would consider a wine list while the sommelier hovered over him.

And then he had an idea.

Maybe there was a fourth option, one that would result in his survival. He'd already beaten six of them, he thought. Be a pity to allow the seventh Specserv clown—and a 21st Century clown, at that—to do him in.

The Corporal still pursued him, intently aiming his gun. Not watching what he was doing, or where he was going.

Jack smiled, and then gritted his teeth and pedaled like mad. Here goes nothing, he thought to himself.

"And that is why we must focus our efforts on revenue," said the gentleman in the black suit.

The lecture hall was filled with over one hundred similarly dressed men, and they all listened carefully to his comments, taking notes as he spoke.

"That is why we must be realistic," he continued. "We must keep our feet on the ground. We cannot let flights of fancy divert us from—"

Suddenly, one of the large windows behind him exploded, with shards of glass flying everywhere. And from the center of the destruction came a flying man.

Jack still wore the harness from his flying machine, pedals underfoot, but his wings had been sheered off by the sides of the window as he crashed into it.

The straps of his harness stopped him short, and he immediately flew backward toward the window again like a whiplash snapping him back. He threw out his arms against the windowsill and caught his balance.

Then he noticed the men in the room, each one staring at him, jaws hanging open. Jack started to wriggle out of his harness as he gave them all a faint nod and a weak smile in greeting.

The moment was broken only by another loud crashing sound just above him. *The Corporal*, thought Jack. But did he make it?

The executives watched Jack climb free of his harness. The remaining framework of the wings made the harness too large to bring inside through the window. He held it awkwardly for a moment as they watched, and then let it fall to the ground.

Smiling politely, he climbed from the windowsill and walked across the back of the meeting room to the door. No one said a word, even after he opened the door and walked out, closing it quietly behind him.

The speaker cleared his throat and the men all turned to give him their complete attention.

"As I was saying..." he continued.

Chapter Twenty-Three

1768

DaVinci burst into the parlor.

His entrance caused a stir amongst the ladies sitting there.

"Why, Signor DaVinci, you honor us!" trilled Miss Annette, the oldest of them and the woman obviously in charge.

The women were already buzzing. There had long been rumors about the appetites of the celebrated Italian, but while he had never visited their establishment, neither had he been found enjoying different tastes. Miss Annette thought he was most likely asexual, at least in recent years. But no one would have expected him to storm into the parlor of the Hellfire Club with a frantic look on his face.

"Excuse me, ladies, please pardon the disruption," he bowed while his eyes scanned the room.

"It is no disruption," Miss Annette smiled. "I hope we may be of service to you."

The other ladies, with bright lipstick and more than a little powder, focused their attention on him. Several of them stood, presenting their goods to the venerable Italian.

"I certainly hope so, Madame," said DaVinci uncomfortably. "You see—"

Miss Annette clapped her hands.

"Come, come girls!" she ordered. "Line up! Let Signor DaVinci have a good look at you!"

The rest of the girls stood up and they all scurried into place, giggling as they lined up for the inevitable review. But this time, the review did not come, and DaVinci demurred.

"You are too kind, but I am afraid that is not why I'm here—" he said.

A couple of the girls looked at each other knowingly and giggled again. Miss Annette admonished them with a glance and they demurely hid their smiles behind their hands.

"But please!" she smiled. "Give us a chance to satisfy you. It will be our privilege."

"Again, you are too kind, but I am only here seeking information," he said politely, then lowered his voice. "Actually, I am looking for someone."

Miss Annette furrowed her brow in concern.

"Oh, Signor, I mean you no disrespect, but I hope you will understand that in our profession, we must utilize the greatest discretion," she said.

"Madame, this is a very serious matter," he said with a more serious edge to his voice. "It is, in fact, a matter of life and death."

She raised an eyebrow.

"I—well, I don't know," she said uncomfortably. "Just who is it you're looking for?"

He paused for a moment, then lowered his voice.

"Dr. Franklin," he told her.

He saw several of the girls react. Franklin had either been here very recently or was still secreted away upstairs, he decided.

"Dr. Franklin," she said, taken aback and not sure how to respond.

"Yes," said DaVinci. "I know this is one of his favorite—establishments, and it is most urgent that I find him."

"I—I'm afraid I haven't seen him—" she stammered.

"No, but if you had, you couldn't tell me," said the Italian. "Isn't that correct?"

"Yes," she answered. "I mean—no—"

"Madame, I'm sure you would not wish to go down in history as the woman who murdered Dr. Franklin—"

"Murder!" she answered with a pained expression.

"Or the person who doomed the British Empire—"

Miss Annette heaved a sigh.

"Which room is he in?" he asked straightforwardly.

She looked up at him, sadly and resignedly.

"I can't tell you—to go left at the top of the stairs, first door on the right."

The Italian smiled at her, then bowed again.

"Madame, I am in your debt," he said grandly. "Dr. Franklin, your country and myself are all at your service."

With a speed that belied his age, DaVinci straddled the stairs two at a time. When he reached the top, he knocked rather loudly and then threw the door open.

There he saw an extremely embarrassed, fully clothed Franklin, who had thrown a blanket over his head in an attempt to hide. At his side was an extremely unembarrassed, extremely naked woman who made no attempt at all to hide anything from him. DaVinci, on the other hand, was as embarrassed as Franklin but had to pursue his mission. He threw his hand over his eyes as he spoke.

"Please forgive me, Miss, but I need to speak to Dr. Franklin," DaVinci said.

"All right," she said nonchalantly. "Go ahead."

"Signor, please, I assure you," Franklin said, "I am only here seeking refuge. I didn't take those papers. I do not know how they got in my pockets, but Specserv is after me! Eric told me—"

"Will you stop talking?" said the exasperated Italian.

"I admit it! I did take my notebook back, but it was my notebook! Can you forgive me?"

"It's all right," said DaVinci. "There is no need to apologize."

"And now you've caught me!" he moaned, peeking out from under the blanket. "What irony! For stealing my own notebook! I suppose you're going to turn me in to Specserv."

"No," said DaVinci. "I'm trying to help you."

Franklin paused. The slight change in his demeanor was noticeable only to the most careful observer, so DaVinci wasn't aware of anything.

"Oh, of course!" Franklin said as he rolled his eyes. "I forgot. You're my friend! That is why you stole my notebook, took credit for my discoveries, tried to plant documents on me and set His Majesty's troops after me! Because you're my friend!"

A strange look appeared in Franklin's eyes, a look the Old Man had never seen before, almost as if the American had reached his limit.

"It's all right to be a little suspicious—" conceded DaVinci.

In fact, Franklin was fed up. He was tired of being pushed to the breaking point. Now, he was ready to push back.

"Oh, is it?" asked Franklin, dripping sarcasm as he rose to his feet. "Thank you so much for your permission, you bastard!"

"Excuse me?" asked the Italian.

"You heard me, you dago son of a bitch!" said Franklin, his anger starting to overwhelm him. "I am sick and tired of it, sir! My parlor is in rubble, my reputation has been slashed to bits, and Specserv is after me, and it's all because you're my friend!"

As he finished speaking, he slowly stood and then lunged fiercely at the Old Man, grabbing him around the neck with both hands.

"Stop—" gasped DaVinci as he struggled to break free. "Choking—me—"

Both men were in surprisingly good shape for their ages, and while the Italian got his hands away from his neck long enough to catch a breath, the American quickly latched on again.

They stumbled around the small room for a moment, and then the woman, who was becoming more and more unnerved by the scene played out before her, leaped up at both of them.

"Stop it!" she ordered. "Stop this right now, you two, or I shall have to call Madame Annette!"

The men continued wrestling, so the naked woman did her best to jump between them and break it up.

"I'm warning you two!" she barked as she tried to separate them.

It was a sight that would perplex most historians; Leonardo DaVinci, the most brilliant man of the Italian Renaissance, and Benjamin Franklin, statesman, inventor and author, wrestling with a naked prostitute in a whorehouse in Victorian London.

Fortunately, the nude woman proved to be instrumental in breaking up the brawl. After she positioned herself between the two men, neither was brazen enough to lunge for the other across her undraped body. Finally, she simply pushed them apart.

"Easy, easy!" she warned. "Are you going to be good boys? Or are you going to be naughty?"

She spoke the last words with a definite tone in her voice, and walked over to a dresser. On the top of it was a black leather riding crop, and another leather device that DaVinci could not identify. But the riding crop alone was sufficient.

"No no!" interjected the Old Man. "Good! We're going to be good."

Was he wrong, or did Franklin look slightly disappointed? No matter. He was much too old for this sort of nonsense, he decided.

"Yes, good boys..." sighed Franklin.

"Then I'll leave you two alone," she said, slipping into a tiny robe and opening the door. "But if I hear you misbehave again..."

The remainder of her threat was implied but unspoken, and she stepped into the hallway, closing the door behind her.

"Nice girl," murmured DaVinci.

"Helps me work off tension," said Franklin. "She's marvelous. That's why I come here."

"Of course," said DaVinci, walking over to a chair and sitting.

"Are you going to bring me in?" asked Franklin.

"No," said DaVinci.

"Then may I go?" he asked. "If you can find me this easily, then it surely won't be long before Specserv catches me."

"I need your help, sir," said DaVinci.

It was the last thing Franklin expected to hear from the Old Man at that point; he was sure their relationship had deteriorated to the point of open warfare.

"Well—what do you mean, sir?" he asked, truly confused.

And with that, DaVinci told him the entire story. He explained what he had heard at the cabinet meeting, and how the Minister of Peace and Lord North were planning to mount a campaign of global terrorism that would result in an Anglo Empire that would control the world. He related their plans to deal with the "undesirables" that stood in their way and the brutal manner in which they would deal with them. It wasn't until he began describing their weapons of destruction that the white-faced American responded.

"A-automatic firing machine guns?" he gasped. "Electric-powered tanks? Armies in flying machines? B-but those sound like—like—"

"Like some of our own inventions?" asked DaVinci.

"Well—yes!" blurted Franklin.

"I'm glad you were paying attention," said DaVinci, who then felt a sudden twinge of guilt over his sarcastic tone. "They used our work, our plans, our discoveries, to make their weapons of war. But they didn't tell us about them until they were already built."

"Maybe—they didn't want us to stop them in case we had second thoughts," mused Franklin.

"They used us!" said DaVinci, getting more agitated. "They used us and manipulated us, and after they took everything we were willing to give them, they decided to take the rest. Well, they're going to be getting tired of us rather quickly if—when we stop giving them new toys."

"But what can we do about it?" asked Franklin. "He is the king—"

"We must find a way to stop them," said DaVinci, formulating his thoughts as he spoke—he had not actually considered their future actions much beyond that point. "If not here, then in the America, and the West Indies, and the Far East! We need to recover the rest of our designs, if only to make certain that they do not fall into the wrong hands!"

"B-British hands?" stammered Franklin. This was still too new to him, and despite the recent events, was requiring an adjustment in his thinking.

"That is correct," DaVinci answered. "We can trust no one. But first, we have to get all of our designs back!"

Franklin pulled out his pocket watch nervously, and with trembling hands flipped open the cover.

"I'm afraid that will be impossible," he informed the Italian.

"What are you talking about?"

"My notebook—my most important notebook, the only one with the latest unseen designs—is leaving for Baltimore at any minute."

"What?"

"I gave them to the captain, with strict instructions to deliver them to a friend in Pennsylvania," he explained. "I-I too wanted to deliver them to the Americans."

"Do you know the captain? Are you certain you can trust him?"

"Well—I've sailed with him before."

"What ship?"

"The *Periwinkle*."

DaVinci turned toward the door and Franklin stood, grabbing his right shoulder to stop him.

"Wait! Where are you going?"

"I have to get them back."

"Let me come with you!" begged Franklin.

"No. You stay here. Too many people know you—and too many of them are looking for you."

The Old Man threw the door open and began walking downstairs, his wide strides taking two steps at a time. Franklin waddled behind, trying to cajole, coax and flatter him into changing his mind.

"We'll go straight to the docks."

"Too risky."

"I'll wear a disguise."

He looked at the ladies watching from the parlor and his eyes caught bits of clothing hung near the bottom of the stairs.

"I can dress like a woman!" he pleaded.

DaVinci wrinkled his nose.

"Too obvious. You need to stay back, stay away from me, or you'll get us both captured. I can only do this if I act on my own!"

Franklin stopped in his tracks. The Old Man was right, but something in his insistence didn't sit well. He watched as DaVinci pushed the door open and stepped out into the street.

The American looked down into the parlor. There were still a few consolation prizes, he supposed. Several were smiling at him and he winked back at them.

"Don't worry, ladies," he grinned. "I'm not going anywhere."

No sooner were the words out of his mouth than the door was thrown open again.

For a moment, he thought it might be the Old Man returning, having had a change of heart. Then his eyes grew wide as four men stepped inside. They glanced around the foyer quickly, watching as the women in the parlor scrambled off, and then looked up at the staircase where he was standing.

Specserv.

Four of them. His eyes met theirs and he knew the jig was up.

"Dr. Franklin!" snapped the one in front. "We shall have to ask you to come with us."

The American heaved a sigh.

"Yes. Yes, of course," he nodded sadly.

He considered running away, but he was simply a little too old for that sort of thing anymore. Or was he?

"Frankly, you arrive just in time," Franklin told his captors. "The depravity of this house is unequalled. Why, even in that room next to you—"

The door nearest them was open a few inches. The men shuffled their feet, edging closer to peer inside the room. As they nonchalantly craned their necks in hopes of spotting some delicious depravity, Franklin suddenly spun on his heels. With a speed that belied his age, he dashed to the end of the hall, pushed the door open, and scrambled to the window. Behind him, he could hear the soldiers scrambling up the stairs.

Giving a quick wave to the lady and the undersecretary who were busy copulating, he ran across the room and threw himself out the second-floor window, all the while with only one thought on his mind.

DaVinci. Was the man who had betrayed him throughout the years, betraying him once again?

Chapter Twenty-Four

1768

The Old Man hurried through the streets as quickly as his spindly legs would carry him. The docks were nearby, and he was determined to get there in time. The streets seemed to be bustling with activity, and he had to weave through the townsfolk. One or two of them may have recognized him—he wasn't sure—but no one reacted with alarm, and there was no indication that he was being pursued.

The docks appeared to be fairly quiet when he finally reached them. He peered around frantically, trying to spot a likely looking ship, one that seemed ready to cast off. Other than one which had apparently just docked, there was no noticeable activity.

He approached the sailor closest to him.

"Pardon me," he said, trying to disguise his still thick Italian accent. "Could you tell me where I might find the *Periwinkle?*"

The old sailor studied him for a moment, then turned to his right, squinted, and pointed off into the distance.

"Yep," he answered. "That'd be her, right there."

DaVinci looked. Perhaps 500 yards downriver, in the middle of the Thames, sailed a large vessel. It was too far for the Old Man to see any identifying signs, but there was a sinking feeling in the pit of his stomach when he laid eyes on it.

"Not movin' too fast, though," the Sailor muttered. "Ya could almost catch 'er..."

His words shocked the Old Man back to his senses.

"Thank you!" he said, and started scurrying off in the direction of the ship.

"Yer not—I was just havin' a joke!" the sailor called to him, then started cackling to himself. "You'll never make it!"

With the *Periwinkle* in sight nearly every second, the Old Man started after her. If there were even the remotest chance he could catch her, he had to try.

The streets that ran along the river were broad and not particularly busy, so the Old Man broke out into a full run. This time, he did attract the attention of many passers-by watching the curious sight. But DaVinci didn't care. He kept up the pace and found himself catching up to the vessel. He hadn't run that hard since the 16th Century, and his lungs were feeling the burn. He tried to ignore the pain and concentrate. Concentrate on putting one foot in front of the other, he thought, and just keep doing it.

He tried to put his legs on automatic and focus his mind on other things. Exactly why was he doing this? He had a rather good life right now. He was a court favorite, even though he couldn't shake the feeling he was being used. So what? He had a warm bed and a roof over his head, and the finest meals in Britain. All he had to do was design a few lethal toys now and then, and he could live out the rest of his life as a pampered royal pet. And if they used his designs to exterminate a few—no, no—to defend the Empire, then wasn't that fair? They were living up to their part of the bargain, weren't they? Then why did he feel so awful about it all?

The ship was only a hundred yards away now. As DaVinci ran, he was struck by another thought. After he catches it— what then? It won't stop and pull over just because he asks. All of his plots, designs and schemes were conflicting with each other and confusing him. There was only one thought that he was completely sure of: this plan was not very well thought out.

Fortunately, the crew had not yet unfurled all of the sails. They couldn't build up much speed until they had moved a little farther from the harbor traffic. The result was that the ship was moving much slower than normal, and it was easier for the septuagenarian to catch up to it.

And catch it he did. DaVinci found himself on the bank of the river, trotting along to stay even with the vessel, unsure what to do next. They would have been a stone's throw away if his arm had been in peak throwing condition, he decided. Instead, he tried the simplest approach.

"Ahoy!" he shouted. "Over here!"

None of the crew on deck looked up. Unfortunately, this was not too surprising, as he correctly assumed that the wind and the water had drowned out his shouting. He desperately tried to think of a way to get their attention.

The Old Man looked down, hoping to find a rock of sufficient size to throw, but small enough to travel a fair distance. But there was nothing but grass and mud at his feet. His lungs continued to ache, and he began to worry. He couldn't continue even this more leisurely pace for long. He needed a rock, but another scan of the ground disappointed him again.

"Think," he muttered. "Isn't necessity the mother of invention?"

No sooner did the words leave his lips than he gave a start. Was that one of Franklin's?

As he trotted along, he once again noticed the jingling of coins in his jacket, coins that had weighted down the right side of his jacket.

Of course! He reached inside and pulled out a two-shilling coin, just the right size and weight. He paused for a moment, then hurled it toward the ship with all his strength. The coin sailed through the air in a perfect arc, landing precisely where he wanted it—on the main deck, just a few feet away from one of the crew. He watched as the sailor looked up, puzzled, and looked around the deck. Then, he looked toward the shore and saw the Old Man frantically waving his arms as he jogged along the bank to keep up with them. In fact, as they approached a bend in the river, the Old Man had no trouble staying ahead of the *Periwinkle*.

The sailor spoke to another of the crew, and they both walked over to the ship's railing. The sailor who had first heard the coin smiled and gave a brief wave, then started to turn back.

"Ahoy!" called DaVinci again, gesticulating frantically. "I need to come aboard!"

The two men strained to hear his cries.

"What?" asked the second sailor.

"I need to come aboard! Now!" shouted DaVinci.

"Sorry, mate!" shouted the first sailor. "You're a little too late!"

"But it's very important!" pleaded the Italian.

DaVinci turned his head back to see the riverbank, and saw a small cliff ahead, overlooking the river by about twenty feet high and blocking his path.

"Nothing we can do, mate!" shouted the second sailor. "We can't steer the boat over to you, now, can we?"

Left with no choice, the Old Man began scaling the rock in front of him, which rose up from the ground at a 45-degree angle.

"Wait! You can't leave!" he shouted as he climbed. He had to keep their attention on him or there was no hope.

As he was looking at them, disaster struck. He stepped on a rock that twisted his right ankle, sharply and painfully.

"Arghh!" he cried.

He tried putting weight on it, but excruciating pain shot up his leg and he immediately jerked it away. He looked up, only a few feet from the top of the cliff. Clenching his teeth and holding his right leg away from danger, the Old Man slithered the rest of the way to the top of the cliff. As he sat on top of the giant rock and saw the *Periwinkle* about to pass by him for the last time, he realized that it was now or never.

He clambered to his knees and crawled to the edge. With his weight entirely on his left leg, he stood up, shouted "Here I come!" and dove into the river.

The Old Man never considered himself a strong swimmer, and normally avoided the water. But in the heat of the moment, he didn't stop to think about it.

Luckily for him, the water was the best place he could have put his ankle. Although he certainly couldn't walk on it, he had no trouble swimming with it; whatever intermittent pains came shooting up his leg only gave his swimming an increased urgency. The winds had died down and the *Periwinkle* almost seemed to be standing still.

The men on deck watched as he paddled closer. It wasn't long before the strain and his feeble swimming skills began to tell. He had jumped in fully clothed, and his now-waterlogged garments were pulling him down. It was a struggle just to stay above water, he thought to himself. He stopped his efforts for a moment, just to see if he would be able to float, and began sinking. It was simply getting too difficult, and he was old and tired.

The Italian took a few more kicks, but began sinking once again. If he had to die, then drowning was a reasonably painless way to do it, he decided, and resolved to approach the final mystery with as much dignity and intelligence as he had approached everything else in his life.

As his head dipped below water once again, he determined to simply give in, take in a few lungfuls of water, and it would all be over before he knew it. All of the aches and pains, all of his worries and concerns. He sucked in his first breath of water.

And he immediately began choking. It was not a pleasant sensation. Had he really read that drowning was one of the better ways to die? How the devil did they know, he thought angrily. This was not pleasant. And, it did not seem quick. In fact, this underwater world appeared to be stuck in slow motion. He did not want to go out coughing and vomiting, loosening his bowels and bladder and ending up as turtle food.

In the end, it was the pure indignity of the whole situation that inspired him.

He summoned up his last reserves of energy and kicked, waving his arms with as much strength as he had left. It was enough to push him toward the surface one more time. And when his nose and mouth broke the water, he began coughing violently, forcing out as much water as he could. But too late, DaVinci realized that it was all the energy he had in reserve. Well, at least he didn't give in without a fight, he thought with some consolation.

Completely drained, the Old Man started to sink one final time. How very odd, he thought as he started below the surface, perhaps the sea legends are true. He was going down for the third time, and it was going to be the last time.

He felt the belt of his coat floating between his fingers, and remembered thinking that if he had peeled off his clothes before jumping in the river, he might have lasted a bit longer. Of course, he was beyond that now. He closed his fingers around the belt, and was surprised to find that it gave him a tug. Though he was nearly beyond earthly concerns, he wondered what the devil was pulling on it. Could it be a fish? A turtle?

The Old Man somehow kept hold of the belt. It began pulling him up, and when he cleared the surface, he coughed a couple more times and grabbed the lifeline with his other hand, as well. It continued pulling him, and he found himself being slowly dragged along the surface of the water.

If he'd had more energy, he might have noticed that it was a rope, rather than a belt. As it was, he was so glad to be breathing air again, he didn't care.

On the other end of the line, the two sailors were hauling him in as quickly as they could. The Old Man had appeared oblivious to their shouts, and they'd had to toss the rope three times before it finally became tangled in his fingers.

They hauled the Old Man aboard ship, while his rescuer scrambled up the rope ladder and joined them.

"Is he breathing?" asked one of the sailors gathered around him. Another pulled his shirt up and put his head to the Old Man's chest and listened.

"I think so," he answered.

The question was further settled when the Old Man coughed violently, then turned his head slightly and vomited up a belly full of water. The sailors reacted with all the refinement of men of the sea used to such matters. They wrinkled their noses and quickly backed away; the sailor who had been listening to his breathing peeled off his shirt in disgust.

"Ugh!" he said distastefully. "This is my best shirt! Let him drown, for all I care!"

But DaVinci had apparently passed out on the deck. He would live, though none of the crew seemed especially happy about it. A few sailors came closer to have another look.

"What'll we do wif' 'im?" asked one.

"Should we take 'im inside?" wondered another.

"We'll have to swab the deck after we move 'im!" said a third sailor. "'E's gone and spewed all over it!"

Suddenly, the group stepped back and formed a path for another man.

"What's all this?" snarled the grizzled, elderly Captain Sparks.

"We just pulled 'im aboard, sir," offered one of the crowd.

"We ain't even made it to sea yet!" snapped the Captain. "Where the devil'd he come from?"

The sailors crowded around the body began to tell him the story, at least as well as they knew it. The two sailors who had initiated the rescue slunk away. Though they had once harbored vague thoughts of being cited for their heroism, it now appeared more likely they would be keelhauled for hauling garbage onto the vessel.

When the story was finished, the Captain looked down at the unconscious body.

"We can't be haulin' everybody aboard what gets washed up here," he said. "We got no room for passengers, particularly non-payin' passengers. 'Sides, he looks dead to me."

The others stared at the body. There was a slow but perceptible rising and falling of the chest, but they knew what their Captain wanted to hear.

"Yeah, looks dead to me, too, Captain," said one of them.

"Stone dead," said another.

The others all murmured their assent, and the Captain looked rather pleased.

"Well, if he's dead, we ain't gonna be hauling him all the way to Baltimore, now, are we?" he asked in a tone that suggested he was talking to a group of uncomprehending imbeciles. It was the usual tone he used to address the crew, and it seemed to work well.

"Uh...no sir?" ventured one.

"That's right," he answered.

"So what do we do with him, Captain?" asked another one of the crew.

The Captain gave him a look that said "Isn't it obvious?"

"Pitch him over the side!" he snapped, and his men rushed to obey his orders.

Careful to avoid the vomit, four of the sailors dragged his lifeless body to the railing above the Thames and dropped it into the murky waters. And there ended the brilliant career and magnificent life of Leonardo DaVinci.

THE END OF *THE TIME AUTHORITY BOOK ONE*

The first adventure of Stan and Jack concludes in *The Return of The Time Police: The Time Authority Book Two*

ABOUT THE AUTHOR

Kim "Howard" Johnson has written comic books for Marvel, DC and Event Comics. He is a director of improvisational comedy, an actor, and is rumored to hang around with the Monty Python gang. Howard's other books include *The Return of the Time Police: The Time Authority Book Two, Monty Python's Tunisian Holiday, The Funniest One in the Room, The Dare Club: Nita, The First 280 Years of Monty Python,* and he is co-author of *Truth in Comedy* and *The Dare Club: Nita.* He lives with his wife Laurie, son Morgan, and boxers Comet and Astro.